DOGS IN THE MOONLIGHT

BOOKS BY JAY LAKE

Green Grow the Rushes-Oh (chapbook)
Greetings from Lake Wu (collection)

Edited
(with Deborah Layne)
Polyphony 1
Polyphony 2
Polyphony 3
Polyphony 4

DOGS IN THE MOONLIGHT

JAY LAKE

PRIME BOOKS

Prime Books
an imprint of **Wildside Press**
www.prime-books.com
www.wildsidepress.com

Hardcover ISBN: 1-930997-56-6
Paperback ISBN: 1-930997-57-4

This one's for my mother and her goats, along with Vicki, Mikal and all the good people of the real Caldwell County. And with thanks to Wordos, TL and everyone who helps.

CONTENTS

INTRODUCTION

RAY VUKCEVICH

The stories in this volume are grouped under the headings *Ghosts, Angels, Gods*, and *Aliens*, but they are all about Texas. Jay Lake is working firmly in the tradition described in that famous quote Pat Conroy attributes to his mother. "All Southern literature can be summed up in these words: 'On the night the hogs ate Willie, Mama died when she heard what Daddy did to Sister.'" (Pat Conroy in *Book-of-the-Month Club News*, Dec 1986).

There are more goats than hogs in these stories, and there is a bird talking to the bones of a murdered woman. There is a dead angel out in front of the doublewide, many kinds of intoxicants, a raccoon, and Southern fried rock. Elsewhere you'll encounter a reptilian rainbow angel, big storms, strange eggs, and the bacon-headed kid. You'll find beanie-weenies and Wonder Bread and diet Dr. Pepper. Down at the Coon Dog Lounge, they served *both* kinds of beer (Lone Star and Shiner). And you'd be disappointed if there were no wood chipper. You won't be disappointed.

Jay Lake writes with a gutsy, confident energy that never fails to sweep readers up and carry them along to the end of the ride. The fact that many of these stories appear here for the first time will be a happy surprise for Lake fans.

In the title story, "Dogs in the Moonlight," Bet Method comes down the hill to see what the ruckus is about at Ralph's place and finds out something has killed Ralph's Dogs. . . . Ralph's got all the Texas hill country stuff going for him including too much drinking and a missing wife. Bet mentions the Chupacabras. Things get ugly. And funny. And spooky. In fact, "ugly, funny, and spooky" is a good way to describe most of these stories.

Things have gone terribly wrong in "The Oxygen Man." This is Texas after the "biosphere crash," and everyone needs what the Oxygen Man sells, but not everyone can afford it.

"The Goat Cutter" is probably an underground classic by now. Readers will be happy to have it collected again here. I suppose those of us who do not live in Texas but who nonetheless suffer now and then when Texan politics spills over on us should not be surprised to learn the Devil lives there, but what he's up to with an old school bus covered with Bible verses written in goat's blood is a big surprise.

While looking for arrowheads in "Ancient Wine," a man crawls into a cave and finds a god who talks him into buying more Mad Dog and going cruising for chicks in a Cadillac. . . . Why not? It's Texas.

And who do you suppose is "Hitching to Aurora"? I can't tell you. It's just too funny.

So, that's right, I'm not from Texas, and while I hate to contradict Lyle Lovett, Texas probably doesn't want me anyway. I used to think the Lone Star state couldn't be too different from rural Arizona where I grew up, but now that I've read Jay Lake's Texas stories, I know better. . . . It's time to read the stories yourself.

I hope you have as much fun as I did.

GHOSTS

DOGS IN THE MOONLIGHT

One fine April evening shooting broke out down the hill from me.

I'm pretty firearms-averse, but that sort of thing gets your attention. Ralph Lazard, my only near neighbor, doesn't have much use for me, and I've got mixed feelings about him at best, but neighbors look after each other out here in the Texas Hill Country.

So I waited about ten minutes after the shooting stopped, then push-started my '75 Volvo sedan. The car rattled slowly down the half-mile or so of steep gravel track as I went to see what was wrong. I came sputtering around the stand of mesquite just outside Ralph's front gate to find the man himself waving a thirty-ought-six at me.

"God damn, Bet!" he yelled, lowering the rifle barrel to point at the dirt.

Better Method, that's me, raised in a school bus by a couple of dropouts with a lot of LSD and not much sense. It hasn't been easy being a boy named 'Bet,' but my sister Crystal definitely got the worst of it.

I killed the headlights but left the engine running, and got out of the car.

"Ralph, you okay?"

We nearly had a full moon, and the stars are always bright out here in Kerr County, so I could see Ralph clearly. He was a big old man with a battered face and a life to match. For all that it was about fifty degrees, he was sweating like he'd been out postholing. The gun trembled in his hands, rattling against the bottle of Shiner Bock he'd got in the crook of two fingers. Ralph wore one of those old man polyester jump suits, and reeked of perspiration and beer.

"You seen anyone on the road?"

"No." It was a silly question—I lived at the upper end of our little road. No one drove between his place and mine but me.

"You didn't see no taillights or nothing heading down for the highway?" He sounded desperate.

"Sorry, Ralph. Um . . . why don't you put that gun down and tell me what's going on?"

"My dogs." Ralph swung the gun toward the dark woods. "Some crazy son-of-a-bitch cut up my God-damned dogs." He choked back a sob, then loosed another round off into the night.

"The gun, Ralph." I held out my hand. I don't usually handle firearms, but it seemed time to make an exception.

#

We stood out by the dog run, me holding the rifle and Ralph holding his Shiner Bock. Three coon hounds were dead at our feet. It was gory, even by moonlight.

"Tore their throats out. God damned kill zone." He rolled the neck of the bottle in his big fingers. "I've seen stuff like this done with a k-bar, in country, but never here Stateside." The beer bottle shattered in his hand. I jumped, startled. Ralph didn't even seem to notice.

Ralph didn't have a lot left to notice. His wife had left him a year or so after I moved into the area—right about this time of year in fact, on their wedding anniversary. People said she was tired of rusty pickups and droughts, broiling summers and scrawny cattle.

I knew she was tired of Ralph, especially, because she told me so personally, with great care and attention, shortly before she ran off with a stock boy from the H.E.B. grocery in town. They stole a fast car and headed west. And Marion especially hated his dogs. Perversely, they had always loved her.

As if that wasn't bad enough, a couple of years after that, Ralph's boy Leroy got run down and killed by a Chevy Suburban filled with drunken starters from the high school football squad. Kerrville had a shot at going to state that year, so there wasn't much community interest in serious efforts at prosecution. Ralph's marriage hadn't been worth the effort to his wife, and Leroy's life hadn't been worth the effort to the county attorney.

All Ralph had now was his dogs, and fools like me on whom to lavish his resentment. And someone had just taken his dogs.

I was glad as hell he never found out about me and Marion.

#

We provided ourselves with Shiner Bock from an ice chest. As he started to talk, Ralph cleaned his bloody fingers with splashes from the newly opened beer and an oil rag from the back seat of my Volvo, studying the cut dogs in the orange glare of the car's parking lights.

"I was inside when I heard Dimwit whining." Ralph sniffed and paused for a slug of Bock. "Dimwit, he barks, but he don't—didn't—whine much. He was carrying on pretty loud, so I stuck my head out the screen door. Someone was down here in the pen."

"Weren't they barking?"

"No, it was a person."

Lord love a duck. As far as I could ever tell, the damned animals barked at anything that moved and most things that didn't. Same as Marion, they liked me even though I didn't like them very much. My feelings aside, they sure as hell didn't deserve this.

"The *dogs*, Ralph. Weren't they barking at all?"

He shook his head. "Just Dimwit whining. It was like he knew the—the guy. So I cussed real loud, and . . . "

"And?"

Ralph shifted, looked uncomfortable. I could swear he was shivering. "I never seen nothing like it," he finally said.

The man had spent eighteen months of his youth in the jungles of Southeast Asia killing people, and he was losing control *now*?

17

"He—it—that thing . . . it didn't top five foot six. Its eyes were glowing. And Bet, I swear it had *wings*. Like an angel or something. It tore the throats out of the three meanest coon dogs in the county without them giving any kind of a fight."

"Chupacabras?" I whispered. My one regular magazine was *Fortean Times*. I wasn't even sure who the governor was these days, but I was up on a lot of odd phenomena. Including the distinct possibility Ralph was lying—he was acting damned twitchy. On the other hand, who wouldn't be, finding something like this in their front yard?

"What?" Ralph prompted me.

"Goat sucker," I said, as if that explained anything to Ralph.

"Bet," he said in that tone of voice the good old boys reserve for the contemptibly stupid. "These here are *dogs*, not goats."

#

Out here among the dry creeks and crumbling stock tanks, the world is brown with flashes of dark green, and it always smells like dust and cow shit. We're surrounded by rolling limestone hills, cedar and mesquite, whitetail deer, javelina, turkey vultures, red-tailed hawks, cows and country people. There isn't much for a would-be hippie with a tiny trust fund to do except drink a little beer, smoke a little grass, and read up on the wide, weird world.

So I rooted through my pile of *Fortean Times* until I hit pay dirt. Chupacabras—the story started in Puerto Rico, a culture virus that spread all over Latin America within a couple of years. Sort of a junior version of a cattle mutilator—tearing throats, sucking blood and spreading panic among the *campesinos*.

I believe in a lot of things against all evidence or pressure of public opinion—the brotherhood of man, the power of faith to move mountains, the incompetent evil of Ronald Reagan—but I couldn't bring myself to believe in chupacabras. Not in broad daylight in the Texas Hill Country.

Ralph had refused to go get the sheriff—a combination of stubborn pride and redneck resentment of authority. He wanted to handle this himself. Himself and me and a fearsome bloody dog killer, one happy family on our little hill.

I went out on my porch to watch the view and think about dog killing for a while. After a bit, I noticed a new stain on the decaying white paint of my Volvo, one that seems to be attracting flies. On closer inspection, I realized there were several bloody handprints around the trunk lid. Ralph must have gotten the stuff on the car the night before.

Sighing, I tore a strip of paisley upholstery from my porch couch and went to clean the blood off.

#

Around two in the morning I woke up to barking. It sure sounded like Ralph's dogs were loose again. That struck me as wrong, then I remembered why.

They were dead.

No one else lived closer than two miles to me. It had to be another damned pack—they sometimes roamed the hills, killing my chickens and tearing up God knew what else. I hoped like hell these weren't feral.

Between this new pack and the dog killer, I really didn't want to go outside, but they sounded like they were on the property, close to the house. I had to check. I went into the kitchen and considered my cooking knives for a minute before realizing I could barely cut tomatoes, let alone knife-fight a dog pack. I settled on my police flashlight, one of those six battery jobs that could crack a skull. So armed, I stepped outside.

The moon was bright, on its way to the back of the world behind the western sky. The dogs still barked somewhere just down the hill from me, much closer than they should have been unless they were a loose pack—definitely in my yard, although I still couldn't see where they were.

You can tell a lot from a dog's bark. These dogs didn't sound angry, really, and I couldn't hear a fight in progress, so I stepped off the porch and gave a sharp whistle, the kind you use to herd sheep or goats. The barking stopped immediately. I walked around the yard, checking things. Nothing inside the rusted Studebaker, nothing under my Volvo. Nothing in the old metal stock tank lying on its side. As I worked my way toward the gate, I heard whining.

"Come here, boy." I felt foolish, talking to the dark. I didn't know what was out there. Certainly nothing I really wanted to meet. "Come on, where are you?" I whistled a couple more times and slapped my thighs.

I heard panting, and some excited yips, like a dog doing that little dance when they get worked up. I walked over to the gate. "Here, doggie, doggie."

They started barking again like crazy, sounding like they were right next to me, and I still couldn't see them. They sure did sound like Ralph's dogs, though. One hand on the gatepost, I swept the flashlight across some Johnson grass and post oak. When something cold nudged my temple, I screamed.

"What the hell you diddy-bopping around here in the hot zone for, Bet?" Ralph had the barrel of his rifle stuck in my right ear. I couldn't see him at all. "Noisy bastard like you wouldn't last ten minutes in country."

"Me? What the hell are *you* doing?!" I was mad enough to grab the rifle barrel, pull it away from my head. "Jesus Christ, don't point that God-damned thing at me again or I'll stick it so far up your ass they'll need a tongue depressor to find it!"

"I heard Dimwit up here," said Ralph real quietly. "Howling and barking with Dummy and Fleabag."

"Ralph." I sighed. "We buried all three of them last night, remember?"

"I heard 'em, Bet." The tears stood out in his voice. I still couldn't see Ralph—he was crouched in the big wisteria by my gate, but his voice shook. "I know their barking. I heard my dogs."

"Ralph," I said in my gentlest voice. "I don't know what we heard, I don't know why. But your dogs are dead and buried. Come up to the house. I'll make some ham scramble and crack a couple of beers."

He stepped out of the shadows of the wisteria into the moonlight. I backed away—Ralph had returned to the jungles of Southeast Asia. He wore torn fatigues, his face blackened with some mucky, dark crap. He was carrying a lot of gear.

"Whoa, Ralph, this is Kerr County, not Da Nang." I really, really hoped he didn't know about me and Marion.

Ralph didn't answer at first, just stalked me as I trudged back up the yard.

"Bet . . . " he finally mumbled from behind me. "If my dogs were going to come back, why'd they come to you instead of me?"

I bit off the first answer that leapt to mind—*because they always liked Marion better than you, Ralph, and she liked me better than you.* I thought of a lot of answers, thought of wives gone and sons dead and lives wasted pounding dirt in the hot, brown Texas hills. A lack of honesty seemed kindest right then.

"Because no one would have believed you, Ralph. Not even me."

Especially not me.

#

We were both somewhere on the far side of drunk, sitting on my front porch surrounded by rows of empties with plates of scramble half-eaten at our feet. I had hidden the rifle inside the house as soon as Ralph was too potted to notice. I figured with the weapon gone, we could work on getting so whacked Ralph wouldn't be tempted to go hunting dog killers in the caliche. My plan seemed a lot safer than finding that gun barrel in my ear again in a few hours.

"Why would a dog come back from the dead?" Ralph addressed his question to the darkened western horizon.

"Hell, Ralph, why would *anyone* come back from the dead?"

"Lots of reasons . . . " He hurled a Bock bottle into the yard. It shattered on a fender of the Studebaker. He still hadn't wiped off the face paint.

"Man, I walk around out there. With my feet, I mean."

"Everyone walks around out there, Bet."

"In *my* yard?"

"In the world, boonierat. You sit still long enough, everyone walks by."

The world according to Ralph. It was profound, coming from a drunken, washed-up dirt rancher. "You're deep, man."

"Not deep enough." Unexpectedly, he started to cry. "The dogs, Bet . . . my dogs . . . "

"I know."

"No. You have no God damned idea." He jumped up out of my second-best chair, knocked it over and broke the scramble-encrusted plate. My grandmother's china, such as it was.

"Damn it, Ralph, I've only got three of those left."

"Come on," he said. "I want to show you something." He staggered over to my Volvo, pawed at the driver's door a couple of times before jerking it open. "You'd better give me a push," he called.

I was too drunk to say no.

#

We crashed through my gate. One of the headlights smashed in the process, dimming our already questionable view of the road.

"Ralph!"

He grinned. "We're hitting the LZ hot and hard, man."

We slammed down the moonlit road considerably faster than I drove it in broad daylight. The beer bottles, loose tools and fencing wire in the back seat clattered and bounced with the lurching of my car. Stark terror got me focused real good, but Ralph was at the wheel and there wasn't much I could do. Yelling only seemed to endanger his concentration. At least the rifle was hidden in the busted chest freezer in my bedroom.

"You ever think ill of the dead?" Ralph screamed over the spewing gravel and bone-rattling lurches of our progress through the dark. Twigs and brush slapped against the sides of the car as we slewed back and forth.

I prayed for dawn, for sobriety, for patience. Ralph was an entire twelve-step program on the hoof. "I'm gonna think ill of you if you don't slow down," I screamed back.

"No, no, you don't get it." Letting go of the twisting steering wheel, his right hand chopped up and down. "You ever curse the dead, Bet? You ever hate someone so much it just got worse when they passed on?"

I tried to give the question a serious answer. "I never hated anyone that much. Richard Nixon, maybe. I don't know."

Ralph shook his head, stared at me in the glow of the dash lights instead of watching the road. His pale eyes gleamed out of his dark face paint. We clipped a cedar with a crumpling screech of metal. The other headlight went out. It was pretty damned dark out there on the hill. The inside of the car reeked of juniper.

"The road, Ralph!"

"Yeah, yeah, roger that." He settled down over the wheel again, squinting forward into the dark as if narrowed eyes could compensate for a lack of headlights. He was driving by the amber glow of the one surviving parking light. "Bet, you poor bastard, you ain't had much of a life. You never cursed the dead, that means you never really loved the living."

Oh Christ, I thought, *he'd popped his twist cap for real now.* As Ralph power-slid my Volvo through his own front gate, I leapt up in my seat. I could swear a dog had just licked my ear.

#

We shot by Ralph's doublewide like we were cruising down the highway, busted through another gate and across his pasturage. Damned near hit a Brangus heifer too, which would have been the end of the road for my long-suffering Volvo.

I'd given up talking to Ralph, mostly because I was afraid of whatever crap he might say next. There was *no way* I was looking into the back seat. Not with that warm dog breath panting in my ear. I held on as we tore through a barbed wire fence line. I heard one of the tires go. The car immediately started to pull hard to the right.

Ralph fought the wheel. "Almost there!" he sang out.

We drove up a steep hill, along a track that clearly hadn't been used in years. Saplings taller than me snapped beneath the front bumper to scrape along the bottom of the car. I could hear topsoil spray from the rear wheels. I'd need new transportation considerably sooner than I had budgeted for. Ralph gunned the Volvo up a little switchback and ran it straight at a bank of brush laying against a limestone cliff face.

"Oh God!" I screamed as I let go of the dash to cover my head.

We crashed through the brush and slammed to halt, a much gentler impact than the solid limestone catastrophe I had expected. The engine died with a muttering cough, followed by the pinging of heat dissipation and the hiss of escaping fluids. I looked up to realize we had pushed through the brush into a cave. The stench of overheated engine and scorched brakes twisted through my nostrils. The remaining parking light showed that my Volvo had rear-ended a Corvette convertible.

"Oh, Ralph."

"*Khong xau.*" His grin seemed tight enough to force his teeth out of his gums and his eyes glittered like an amphetamine overdose.

"Huh?"

"Viet— Never mind. End of the line, Bet. Everything you need to see is right here."

#

"After all I've done for her, she killed my dogs, Bet. It wasn't no chalupa cabana."

"Chupacabras," I corrected automatically. Marion? What *all* had he done for her? Ralph was so far gone it had to be him that killed the dogs.

"Yeah," he muttered. "I knew it was her."

The Corvette had been there a long time. The tires were dead flat, there was a thick layer of grime on the car, and the body in the passenger seat was a leathery sack of bones. It grinned at me above a knitted H.E.B. Grocery golf shirt, the kind stock boys wore. There wasn't a matching body in the driver's seat.

Where the hell was Marion? Had she escaped?

I realized I wasn't likely getting out of here. *Stall*, I thought, *stall Ralph, and think hard.* "Was she, uh, here?"

"Oh, yes." Ralph's chuckle echoed in the little cave. "Until she

24

escaped, and killed my dogs. Gets restless every year around our anniversary."

Their anniversary—the day they married and the day she left him. My knees buckled. He couldn't be serious—no way he'd had Marion living up here these past five years, not in a cave. Marion. My heart ached, for a moment, for both of them. She always hated his dogs—was that all he had left of her in his heart?

"She knew I loved them," he added.

"Ah." I figured if I ran like hell back down the track we came up, and he didn't catch me and break my neck on the way, I could make the highway and flag down a ride into town. Ralph didn't have a phone and neither did I, so that was the only way to get help.

"I lost her boy, and no one got called to account for it."

"What?" Leroy died two years after Marion left. Was he crazy, or was she still around?

"Marion was real angry when Leroy died. She knew it wasn't my fault. But when they wouldn't do nothing to those other boys that killed him, she wanted me to take care of it." He shook his head. "I couldn't do it. No more dead boys, not even for her."

God, I thought. Ralph must have walked up to this cave and talked to his wife all the time. No wonder he was crazy.

"She said I'd killed once, it was easy enough to kill again."

"Once?"

Ralph nodded at the dead stock boy. His nametag read, "**Jason, Serving the Public for 1 Year.**" He didn't smell at all. Ralph laughed. "Her boyfriend. I killed him."

Thank God he didn't know about me and Marion.

Ralph studied the expression on my face, then sucked in a breath. "Oh God, Bet, you think I killed my wife, don't you?" He sounded more hurt than anything else.

Honesty, I told myself. It was honesty that killed the cat, not curiosity, but I had to keep him talking. Was she here or not? Where the hell was she? "Yes, the thought had crossed my mind."

"Bet, you know me. I'm not that kind of guy."

Yeah, right. That's obvious.

He reached down into the foot well of the driver's side of the Corvette and pulled out a long dog chain. "She was fine up here until she broke free last week."

He was for real. She'd been up here all this time. His wife, my one-time lover, chained next to her dead boyfriend. I retched, my throat filling with stinging bile as my thoughts spiraled into horrified panic.

I couldn't make it to the cave mouth before my stomach gave out. Ham scramble and Shiner Bock didn't taste any better coming back through the second time. Outside the cave, invisible dogs bark as I heaved, over and over, crying though my eyes were screwed tight.

#

"Ask not for whom the dogs howl," I gasped through my stinging, stinking puke breath.

"What?" Ralph was becoming more and more dissociated. I could almost see his head floating free of its tethering neck.

We sat on the hood of the Corvette, deeper inside the cave. In the growing golden light of morning that flooded through the broken barrier of brush, I could see stacks of unopened army surplus C ration cases, barrels of water, manacles bolted to the limestone wall of the cave, and the little nickel-plated pistol Ralph had slipped out of his boot before I finished throwing up.

Outside, Ralph's dead dogs howled. I didn't think about Marion, not for a moment. Not me.

"Your dogs, Ralph, they're talking to you."

Ralph waved the pistol in a vague gesture. "They're dead. You helped me bury them, remember?"

"They didn't stay dead."

"Not like my boy," he sniffed. "I miss Leroy."

"Yeah, well, somebody misses Jason there, too."

Ralph gave me a hard look before staring back at the cave wall. Me and my big mouth. How the hell was I getting out of this? I wasn't about to wrestle Ralph for the gun. The dead dog chorus was like a color commentator on sports-talk radio—interesting but meaningless. I figured Jason wasn't going to do anything for me at this late date.

If Marion had escaped and killed the dogs, she was probably hiding somewhere nearby. Then I remembered the blood on the trunk of my car. The lock never had worked.

She was in my trunk.

Marion had to have climbed into the trunk while I was helping Ralph bury the dogs.

Something killed those poor coon hounds, and it sure as hell wasn't me or the stock boy. And Ralph loved those damned dogs too much, for one thing.

Get him to confront her, I thought. That ought to cause enough trouble for me to escape. I felt sick about Marion being chained up here all these years, but whatever was between them now was far beyond me. "Ralph." My voice was quiet, calm. "I need a drink."

"Plenty of water up here," he said dreamily.

I nodded at the Volvo. "Couple of six packs in the trunk." *Like hell.*

The thought of beer brought Ralph back into focus for a moment. He looked at me with narrowed eyes. "I don't reckon they would of made the trip up here, what with all that bouncing around."

Inspiration soared, or flapped in this case. "They're wrapped in some laundry. They might have survived."

Ralph wandered back through the cave, down the length of the Corvette, past the Volvo, to the brush-strewn entrance. He staggered a bit, looking confused. I wondered if he was having a stroke. Outside, the dogs kept howling.

He stopped behind the Volvo as I stood up to stare across the two cars at him. I ignored Jason's permanent grin to focus on Ralph's increasingly glassy stare.

"Maybe she is and maybe she isn't," he said.

Marion? "Is or isn't what?"

"You learn weird shit in country."

"Weird how?" He was gone, way far gone. *Keep him talking*, that had to be good. *Be cool about the trunk*, I reminded myself, *don't spook the man.*

"There was a Cuban guy in my platoon, used to slice open chickens and spit rum all over the place. Didn't save him from being killed by a beer truck in Saigon, but it did keep the VC bullets away."

The dogs quieted down as Ralph spoke. Perhaps they were soothed by his voice.

"He showed me the line that separates the living from the dead, Bet. He showed how that line could be moved. Thing is, I did kill Marion." I noticed the Volvo rocking on its shocks. He tapped the trunk lid, tears tracing pale gray lines through his black face paint. "Thing is, then I brought her back. Bet, I loved my wife so much I brought her back from the dead. But she still didn't love me, even after all I done for her."

Dead? Brought back? Had he chained a corpse to the Corvette? I heard the squeak of the Volvo's distressed suspension. Whoever—whatever—killed the dogs was in there. My skin felt cold and numb and my gut threatened to heave again. Dead or alive, suddenly I wanted nothing to do with whatever Marion had become. I didn't want Ralph to open the trunk, not even to save my own life.

Tears, modern tears, tracking over the camouflage face paint of a war lost thirty years ago, focused me back on Ralph. Things had gone so very badly wrong in his life. He needed help, a lot of it.

"Ralph," I said, repenting of my plan. I had to get him, and me, away from the cave and Marion. "I don't need that beer. You don't need to open that trunk. You and me, we could just walk down to town together and check in to the hospital. Leave the cars here, no one would ever know."

The sheriff, I thought, *let him come find Marion.*

"I'd know." Ralph cocked his pistol. "She'd know." He reached for the trunk release. "The dogs would know." Gun ready, he opened the trunk. "Happy anniversary, baby."

The howling rose to merge with a human scream. Something man-sized and leathery sprang out of the trunk, knocking Ralph backward and sideways against the mouth of the cave.

"I love you," he yelled as Marion, naked and desiccated, grabbed him by the throat and face and cracked his head against the limestone. Ralph looked like he was being attacked by a giant, four-legged spider.

I scuttled down the left side of the cars, toward where Ralph was meeting his noisy, messy death at the hands of his late wife. My stomach heaved to the sounds of Ralph's bones breaking against the limestone wall—like hearing sacks of meat dropped on pavement. Marion's chain was caught around my right foot. I kept my eyes on the floor, seeing only Ralph's jungle boots and Marion's curled, dried feet.

And his nickel-plated pistol.

I grabbed that pistol like I was grabbing a snake. I hated the damned things, but Marion had passed beyond killing rage and somewhere into the realm of an elemental force. I stood, my right foot tugged backward by the dog chain and raised the pistol braced in two hands just like in the movies.

Marion dropped Ralph's bubbling body and turned to face me. Everything about her was twisted, curved, pulled tight, her tendons drawn backward in death. Her lips were bacon rind, pulled far back from shattered eggshell teeth, her eyes withered black olives. She looked like a rabid bat weeks dead on the highway.

"Marion." There was nothing to say.

She nudged Ralph with one clawed foot, staring at me. Her body trembled like an overtightened come-along—that killing force was held back, at least for a moment. I noticed that she didn't really breathe. "Finish it," she said. Her voice creaked like my porch in the wind. "Please."

I pulled the trigger, putting a bullet into the chest of my one-time lover, murdering her for the second time in her life as her husband's dead dogs howled.

#

It took a few weeks for the county attorney's office to decide not to charge me. Shooting a corpse wasn't precisely a criminal act, and the sheriff finally chalked Ralph's death up to self-defense on my part. Lucky for me there was no other remotely logical explanation.

I tell myself it all meant something, but I'll be damned if I know what. Nobody got what they wanted, except maybe the dogs. Sometimes those dead dogs come to my window at night, but I just whistle and call them by name, and they whine happily and go away until the next time the moon is bright. Haven't had any problems with roving packs lately, either.

I like to think those dogs are out hunting dead raccoons somewhere in the woods with Ralph and Leroy.

ARRANGE THE BONES

Little ever changed for Elise. Over the years the kitchen's pressed tin ceiling sagged, the ceaseless high plains wind found new passages through the walls, and generations of field mice and feral cats fought across the shattered linoleum. She only wanted to go outside, plant her feet in the red clay soil, and touch the sky. But she couldn't leave her bones, and they couldn't leave the old wood-fired stove where Henry had baked her dry that hot summer day in 1937.

Until the raven came scrabbling down her chimney, found its way into her pile of bone and ash, and thrashed in such panic that the stove door fell open for the first time in almost a century. Rushing through the newly-unblocked chimney, the wind touched her with a hint of freedom.

"Calm in the kitchen," the bird shrieked, voice rustier than the stove's old hinges. "Caught a chance, I did, for quiet." It sighed.

Elise had long ago surrendered her voice to the wind, so it was from the wind that she stole it back. "Hey," she whispered.

"Criminey." The raven hopped around on the stove lids, one beady eye cocked for seeds. "Can't catch a clue from this coop. What could cause such cacophony?"

Elise tried her voice again, steering the wind to a little corner of her will. "You can hear me, bird."

"Pretty bird," spat the raven. "Crams my craw, clumsy casting of stereotype. Call me Cause."

"Cause," whispered Elise. Her voice was getting easier to use. Was strength returning to her ashy old bones? "Cause is reason. Did you come for me, Cause?"

"Cause," the raven said in an unexpectedly normal voice. It dug for mites in one wing, an ordinary bird for a moment, before dragging its black beak out and staring around Elise's kitchen. "Catch who cackling at me?"

"Me," said Elise. Her voice was the creaking timbers of the house, the flap of the last few shingles on the roof, the rustle of the Johnson grass folded against the tarpaper outside. "Call me a ghost."

The bird tapped its beak against the stove lid. "Can't catch a ghost in my claws. Not real."

"No such thing as talking birds, either," said Elise.

"Miracles and wonder. Catch a genome in your hand. Create a cantankerous pet and let it go. Criminey, hand of man made me. Cause *is* effect." The bird choked off a bitter cackle that might have been laughter.

Elise remembered the blows of her husband's axe, the heat of the fire he built in the stove beneath her fresh-cut bones before he'd walked whistling out into the endless llano winds, not even bothering to shut her kitchen door behind him. "Hand of man made me, too," she said in a voice of rattling glass and the snap of old electric wiring. Memories echoed for Elise: the slap of Papa's belly against Mama's to make her be, Elise's aunt slapping her bottom to make her cry, Henry slapping her face to make her stop. Hand of man, indeed.

The bird peered at the stove some more. "Could be old ghost, caught so close."

"Old as the wind, Cause." Elise's voice was the doorknobs rattling. "And twice as tired."

The bird flew around the kitchen in a shuddering explosion of feathers, careening away from the window over the sink, avoiding the open door with its nest of wisteria canes, before settling on the stove again.

"Cause is tired, too," it said. "Can't keep constantly a-wing. Want to be a bird, no more, no less. Creators continue to come for me. No escape."

"And I want to lie beneath the sky," said Elise, the wind down the stove chimney stirring her ashes and carrying tiny pieces of her across the kitchen. "Can you bring me to the sky, Cause?"

The bird hopped up and down. "Can't carry the ghost to the sky. Try to carry the sky to the ghost."

Elise had heard nothing so sweet since she was a little girl. If she still had eyes, she would have wept her joy. "But why?"

"Cause knows being caught forever. Find a way, now." The bird peered around the kitchen, then fluttered over to the counter, hopping among the old tins arrayed there.

"The tall tin," Elise said suddenly, fighting back memories of flame.

The bird knocked the tin over, worried at the lid for a while, then squawked satisfaction. "Cause has caught the way," it said as it picked up a long, splintered match.

"Will you fly away afterwards," Elise whispered in the settling of the foundation, "or will you stay with me?"

"Cause can't carry on forever." The bird flew to the stove, landing precariously on the opened door for a moment. Cause dropped the ancient match on the metal before hopping back inside to gently nudge the bones.

"That tickles," Elise said in the voice of the earth beneath the house. The cats sleeping between the cedar posts of the foundation whined within their dreams.

"Comfort for the ghost," the bird said, brushing tenderly through the ashes, each peck as gentle as a kiss. "Arrange the bones. Respect for the living, respect for the dead."

Back outside the stove, Cause struck the match against the rust-roughened cast iron, then cocked its head to allow the little flame to prosper. The bird took off, flying around the kitchen to set fire to scraps of wallpaper, horsehair insulation, the peeled paint of the pantry door. The raven flew in circles, a tiny, avenging angel carrying fire until the kitchen was a swirling, spiraling torch. The ceiling caught in the hot summer wind, then the roof exploded, a century of dry rot surrendering at once to the flames.

Elise rose into the Texas sky, carried on a column of ash, escorted toward heaven by a burning raven that sung in a rusted voice to match the very choirs of angels.

THE OXYGEN MAN

Even rot takes a long time these days. Outside our window the pale, woody bones of trees still rise high, splintered sponges spearing the sky. Windstorms take them down one by one. Just like something out there took down Papa a few months ago. I searched for weeks as far as my mask and canister would take me into the gloom, but I couldn't never find his body. If I get old enough to have kids, they'll never know a tree at all. Or their Grandpapa either.

"The Oyxgen Man's a-coming," whispers Uncle Raymond from the couch. It's as threadbare as he is, almost his final resting place. His joints are swollen like baseballs to where he can't hardly move, but there ain't nothing wrong with his brain. "Get ready, Bubba."

There ain't no ready to get. We got no way to pay the Oxygen Man. Maybe if he stays away, we won't need our air. Maybe he brings us oxygen starvation the way doctors used to bring people cancer. I press my face to the triple-caulked window, hoping against hope. There is only one price left to pay, and it's too high. "I don't see him."

Outside is black-and-white, like always. Angry dark clouds glow silver at the edges where the sun is hidden, but the rest of the world is flat shadows. Nothing grows now but moss and mold, but there's plenty of dead trees and cruddy canes of old bushes hiding us from the rest of Texas.

Then I spy the light coming toward us. It flickers between tree trunks like hope gleaned behind prison bars. I wish it was Papa, but he's been gone three months now, and this is the Oxygen Man's day. "There he is, Uncle Raymond."

The Oxygen Man always comes on Tuesday. We got to be ready for him. The leaves in our garden tent out back have gone brown and spotty, the plants are starting to stink, and our blood O_2 saturation is low. Already Cissy won't wake up, and Mama cries all the time.

"He's a-coming," gasps Uncle Raymond. "Get ready to pay."

I been the man of the family ever since Papa didn't come home. I go to the air box in the kitchen, where we keep the air counters. They're all the money that is anymore. You can't eat gold, and you can't breathe them old dollar bills. The air box is as empty as it was yesterday, as empty as it's been since I paid every bit of it to the Oxygen Man when he last came calling. Papa's scavenging used to bring home canned food and salvage he could trade to keep air counters in the box, and I ain't been able to replace that.

I ain't much of a man. Now I got to pay for my lack.

#

That light comes bobbing through the trees like Papa's ghost headed home, down the driveway, past the useless tractor and the brittle bones of our last cow. I can see the Oxygen Man in the glow of his light, his tubing all a-sparkle and air rings flashing like water poured from a pitcher. His face hides in the shadow of his wide hat, his plastic mask dark as daylight.

I go to the inside of the airlock, our front door, to greet him. The airlock ain't much, just plastic sheeting duct taped over marine plywood, but it seals the house, more or less. If we had a better airlock, better seals on our windows, the oxygen would last longer, and we wouldn't be as poor. If we weren't as poor, we'd have a better airlock. All I can do is smile and beg. I got nothing else to give him.

The Oxygen Man bangs through the outer door, then stands in the airlock for a moment to let our weather-stripping seal up behind him. I see him through the three little rectangular windows in the old front door. He's exactly as I recollect, a mask of tent sheeting over his face, and hoses run all across his body like he was a thing made of recyclers and fuel cells, except for his clear blue eyes like water in Mama's Dresden china bowl. His hat is wide-brimmed and low-cut, and I know his boots creak when he walks. His knife is well-used and his taser is always close to his hand. He's got air counters strung in little rings all over, each one the worth of a liter of pure O_2. When the Oyxgen Man comes, it's like watching all the wealth in the world walk in the airlock of your house, sit down, and talk to you.

I've heard tell he's from the government, and some people say he's a spirit of the Earth or an angel of the Lord. Uncle Raymond says the Oxygen Man's just a smart son-of-a-bitch who got ahead when the getting was good. All I know is we pay him for us to breathe, and that's the first rule of life. Breathe.

I open the inner door. "Welcome to our home, sir." It's the way you talk to the Oxygen Man. Uncle Raymond learned me that, too.

The Oxygen Man shrugs his way into the house, scuffing his boots on the mud-stained carpet, pulls out an air sampler and stares at it. Just because I'm polite to the Oxygen Man don't mean he's got to be polite to me. "Ambient concentration's dropped to seventeen percent," he finally says. His voice is so ordinary. The Oxygen Man should talk like a preacher, all thunder and fear. "Your blood O_2 saturation must be, what, down at sixty percent of nominal?"

"These are tough times, sir." It's like swallowing my own snot, to be polite to the man who can take our lives by just walking away. Even if I had some way to steal what he had with him, by fists or sly tricks, he'd never come back. No one hassles the Oxygen Man. Not twice. I step to our dinette table, all peeling formica and duct tape, and sit down.

He sits across from me, setting the air sampler next to his right hand. Those clear blue eyes catch me like a knife catches skin. "Two filters like usual?"

I clasp my hands, then open them toward him to show my empty palms. I been practicing that move. "There's nothing left here to pay you with, sir. We need your zeolite filters, to run our oxygen concentrator, but we got no more air counters."

The Oxygen Man glances at my hands, then studies me. Those eyes are ice now, chips of cold trapped in the narrow line of his face that shows above the mask. My heart freezes with them, tight and prickly.

"Air used to be free," he finally says. "But no more."

"Life used to be free," I say, "before the oceans died." Papa and Uncle Raymond call it a *biosphere crash*. We still have air, but the oceans don't put oxygen into it anymore. Most people died when it happened—that's why there's so much salvage in the world now. Me, I can remember being out in green grass under sunlight, when I was little. It's been almost ten years since Papa first closed the airlock door. "But I love my life," I tell the Oxygen Man, "even without the outside. I love Mama, and Cissy, and Uncle Raymond."

He leans forward slightly. "Do you love processed protein base and dented cans of beans?"

That's not what I had expected him to say. "No, sir, I'd rather have the old food, the old ways, but that ain't up to me."

He stares for a moment longer. "You can't bring back the old days and you can't pay your oxygen debt. What will you do?"

I knew he would ask this, just like I know I want to draw my next breath, but the question still sets me back. The answer is worse. "We've got nothing you want." I stare at my hands, which tremble. "Unless you can make use of one of us."

Uncle Raymond grunts softly.

"One of you?" The Oxygen Man is quiet for a moment, as if he expects me to burst into tears. Or maybe flames. "There's men out there who would pay well for a woman. You want to sell one of yours for their amusement?"

This is what I have been wondering—can I sell my sister? My own mother? My breathing grows ragged, and I can't find any words for him at all.

"I didn't think so," the Oxygen Man says at last. "Then bind someone else in your household over to me, and I will credit their life-time value as labor back to you in air counters." He glances at Uncle Raymond on the couch. "For a healthy servant, you could breathe rich air for years." He shrugs. "Or you can suffocate soon. It doesn't matter to me either way. But my time is brief. I have other visits to make."

37

And now the reckoning is upon us. A life of labor—nasty, hard and short I figure. I tap my fingers on the table, one at a time, for each of us. Thumb. Papa's dead. Index finger. Not Uncle Raymond. He can barely feed himself. Middle finger. Mama. She's my mother. Besides, she cries all the time. Ring finger. I know what would happen to Cissy out there in the world. Better to lock her outside now and watch her suffocate in the empty air. Pinkie, but that finger tap turns into a rattling palsy that I cannot stop. I'm the man of the house—this is up to me.

"I'll go," I say quietly. I grab my right hand with my left, jerk it into my lap, grip myself to stillness. A gust of wind rattles our airlock doors. I imagine it is Papa come home, just now, at the last moment, to save the family. "Take me."

The Oxygen Man lays two lithium-exchanged zeolite cartridge filters on the table. "Install one of these while I prepare the contract."

In the hall closet I replace the filter into the house's oxygen concentrator. Behind me I hear the air counters clink onto the dinette table, wealth falling like drips from the hand pump on wellhead. My family will be okay, I tell myself as I check the concentrator's fuel cells, now that they'll have enough oxygen all the time. Mama will smile and Cissy will be full of spit and vinegar and they won't need me every day.

Fingers still trembling, I set the knob to "TEST," overpressuring the oxygen output to break in the filter. Uncle Raymond mutters on the couch. Upstairs, Mama still sobs like always. The hissing of the concentrator fan reminds me of Cissy's breathing as she sleeps her life away. I have bought their freedom with mine.

Even rot takes a long time. I will be years in the Oxygen Man's service—whatever that might mean—or sold to some worse master, working until I become as brittle as the trees. Someday I will die alone and out of breath, like Papa, only no one will come outside to look for me.

Behind me in the front room there is silence. Then a chair scrapes. I hear the airlock door bang. Has the Oxygen Man left without me? Hope against hope, has Papa finally come home?

Bending to check the concentrator's nitrogen exhaust line, I take a deep breath of the almost-pure oxygen leaking from the brass output coupling. I don't want to turn and look behind me. I will never look back.

ANGELS

LIKE CHERRIES IN THE DARK

The angel in Earl's front yard was definitely dead.

Naked and face down, one wing had been torn off, leaving only a bloody stump. The other stood up like a sail, feathers flapping. Those feathers gleamed like an oil slick, and the skin was eggshell white. The angel's hair was a glorious, golden blonde, like Diane who waitressed down at the Coon Dog Lounge dyed hers. Earl knelt, poking at the angel with a busted-off pecan branch.

Behind him, the porch he'd built on their doublewide creaked under Murlene's weight. "Earl, get away from that thing." Her voice was shrill, demanding, everything Earl had come to hate about his wife over the decades.

What had he ever seen in her?

Using the branch, Earl flipped the angel's left hand over. Nice manicure, he thought, sort of like that Kenny Joe who wrangled llamas at the Double D. "Shut up," he said to his wife, as an afterthought.

"I'm calling the sheriff."

She didn't leave the porch, though. Earl reckoned Murlene was eyeballing the angel's tight butt. If it had been a girl's butt, he'd have liked it too. But the golden beard ruffing the jaw put paid to that. He wasn't no Kenny Joe, though Lord knew Murlene could make any man want to switch teams.

Earl stood and walked around the body. Pretty soon he'd flip the angel over, just to see what was there. Given the tight, muscular back-side Earl figured on a pretty good package. He didn't want Murlene getting ideas. "Why don't you get inside and make me some supper, woman?" he said without looking up.

"Earl." Her voice pitched higher. "It might be diseased."

He finally glanced up at his wife. Murlene had on that bright purple muumuu her sister had given her for Christmas, wrapped around three hundred pounds of saggy fat. "Jesus, woman, it ain't no dead vulture. It's an *angel*. Ain't no diseases in Heaven."

Murlene sniffed. "Ain't no murder there either, but somebody done tore his wing off." She stalked back into their trailer, slamming the thin aluminum door.

Earl hated to admit it, but Murlene sort of had a point. He fetched a two-by-four from the shed, laid it across the pecan branch as a fulcrum, and levered the angel's body over. It flopped heavily, landing on the remaining wing to rest at an odd angle, as if being held up by a friend.

Earl shrieked and dropped the board.

Along with the beard, the angel had an enormous penis. And breasts. Perfect, big breasts that stood up like the top of a custard pie, including the little cherry for a nipple.

Earl threw up in the salvia bush. "Damn," he said to himself as he wiped his mouth. "That just ain't *right*."

#

Down at the Coon Dog, televisions flickered on the Nashville Network, NASCAR and football—the holy trinity of a Southern bar with a satellite feed. Sputtering neon advertised both kinds of beer, Lone Star and Shiner. Pool balls clacked in the back, while the floor hissed with peanut husks every time anyone moved. The boys weren't having none of Earl's story.

"What the hell you been drinking, Earl?"

"He's been hitting the formaldehyde again."

"Earl, did Murlene finally fetch you upside the head with something heavy enough to knock some sense into you?"

But he had brought the evidence, by God. Earl opened his rifle case and pulled out a gleaming feather about a yard long.

"It's a sign, boys," he said, waving the feather around like a kootchie dancer. "A sign from God."

Little Big'un McMasters laughed so hard he spit beer all over the bar top. "Earl, you are full of pure-dee shit."

"No, you listen to me, boys. I seen an angel fallen from Heaven, and it was of them he-man-afro-dykes." He poked the feather into the middle of Little Big'un's Army Airborne t-shirt. "God's trying to tell us something about women and men," Earl stage-whispered, "and it ain't *good.*"

"Prove it," said Little Big'un. "That feather ain't nothing. You could'a bought it offa eBay."

Earl waved the feather. "Well, come on then." He grinned at the rest of the boys. "Unless you all are *afraid*. Sissy bastards."

There was a stampede for the parking lot.

#

In the orange glow of the streetlights, the boys from the Coon Dog gathered around the bed of Earl's 1967 Dodge Power Wagon. Earl pulled the bungees from the blue plastic tarp and flipped it back. "See," he demanded.

There was long, horrified silence. Finally, Little Big'un shook his head. "Earl, my friend, you have plum lost it."

They drifted back into the bar as Earl stared after them. He finally looked down into the truck bed. There was a rotting side of beef with a dead vulture atop it, one wing torn off. Shiny maggots squirmed bright in the orange glare.

"Damn," Earl said. He looked at the shimmering feather in his hand, then back at the dead animals. He decided to walk home. A few miles of peace and quiet seemed like a good idea.

#

"Hello, Earl," said Murlene when he finally limped into the trailer. She actually seemed glad to see him, dressed in a decent pants suit instead of that horrible muumuu.

"You look nice." To Earl's surprise, he meant it. He set the feather down on top of the television and picked up the remote.

Murlene patted the couch next to her. "Leave that thing alone and come sit down with me."

A while later, as their clothes dropped to the floor, Earl noticed that feather glowing. Suddenly he knew what it had meant, their private apparition. "There's an angel inside all of us," he whispered to his wife, whose nipples were like cherries in the dark.

"You're *my* angel," Murlene whispered back. Then she licked his ear.

SHATTERING ANGELS

The ceramic angel broke under Bester's heel with a noise like heaven shattering. Random, staccato notes from the skittering fragments echoed off the concrete of the dried-out swimming pool.

Bester stood amid circles of angel figurines on the pool's turquoise floor, flanked by cracked, weed-infested turquoise walls. Broken pool lights stared like blinded glass eyes into the Texas summer heat. He wore nothing but his Dickies overalls and his worst pair of boots—the blunt-toed shit-kickers he used for cleaning septic tanks or slaughtering goats. His big arms were red with sun, gold with tight curled body hair, blue-black with tattoos from Korean alleyways two decades past.

"Momma loves those," said Louisa Sue. Bester looked up at his daughter. She was eleven going on eighteen, wearing cut-off shorts and a halter top he wouldn't dress a twenty-dollar hooker in, with her hair dyed pink.

"Momma's dead," Bester said, his words echoing flat off the pool walls. The funeral would be tomorrow, but he couldn't think that through. Not yet, with the hospital filling his memory like vomit overflowing a bedpan. Bester wiped his eyes, smearing sweat and tears. "Put some clothes on, right now. Girl your age shouldn't even have tits, let alone show 'em off. And that crap you're wearing—it's going in the burn barrel today."

Louisa Sue cocked her head, pink curls dropping over one shoulder. "Da-a-ddy . . . "

Bester grabbed an angel and sent it flying toward Louisa Sue. She ducked, then ran off crying.

He went back to destroying Mavis' prized collection, stomping them into oblivion one by one. He never did find the one he'd thrown at their daughter.

#

One fall day four years later, Bester stepped out of the doublewide looking for Louisa Sue. Their mobile home still overflowed with the avocado and harvest gold look that Mavis had loved. Only the angel shelves in the living room were empty. Nothing else had changed.

Except for Louisa Sue. That damned girl never stopped growing up. There wasn't much Bester could do to keep her behaving right any more. He headed for the barn, out past the empty swimming pool.

Inside, fragments of straw floated in the amber autumn sunlight that spilled through the doors. The musty, sharp scent of the goats washed over Bester, almost relaxing him. Water dripped from a leaky tap, and somewhere nearby a chicken let out a slow, steady cluck.

"Louisa Sue?" Her name came out as a whisper. Bester really didn't want to find his daughter in here, not since she'd started running around with that colored boy from over in Saint Johns Colony. He was afraid of what he would have to do if caught her, and more afraid not to do it. Raising Louisa Sue was too hard, without Mavis to tell him what to do. "Girl," Bester said quietly, "if you're in here, you'd better not be."

Something thumped in the hay loft.

Bester grabbed a shovel. His fingers cramped on the smooth wooden handle as the tool shook in his hand. Using only his left arm, Bester hauled himself up the ladder. "Girl, I hope you're reading a book up there."

He swung himself onto the deck of the hay loft. Bales, both this year's gold and last year's rotting gray. An old feed bucket. One rubber boot. A messy pile of ropes and pulleys. A weathered tarp, folded puffy and big in the corner where the roof sloped down.

Bester heard his own breathing as a rushed rhythm, the heartbeat of the world. He walked across the loft, the wood squeaking with each step, handle of the shovel thumping like a heavy cane. The tarp rustled. He stopped in front of it, nudging a loose corner with the blunt toe of his boot.

His breath echoed so loudly, his pulse pounded so hard, Bester couldn't hear anything else. He reversed the shovel, pointing the blade downward. "Come on out of there," he shouted. His voice sounded like ripping cloth. "You got that worthless *boy* under there with you?"

With the patience, speed and skill that had beheaded dozens of egg-thieving chicken snakes over the years, Bester used the tip of the shovel blade to snag one corner of the tarp and flip it back. "Got you!" he shouted, boot poised for a bone-cracking kick.

One of the barn cats came streaking out. A blind pile of kittens mewed and pushed amid rotten straw within the folded tarp.

Bester collapsed onto his knees, shovel clattering next to him. He folded his arms across his chest as his face prickled up, like fire ants on the move.

"Mavis," Bester whispered. "She's too much for me. I'm trying to raise her right. I can't do it no more."

#

The next afternoon, Louisa Sue was late coming home from school again, so Bester had to make dinner himself. He opened a can of beanie-weenies into a cracked crystal bowl, then laid four slices of Wonder Bread on a pie plate and set out two cans of diet Dr. Pepper. Bester left the Shedd's Spread in the fridge until his daughter made it in. Then he lit a cigarette and sat at the table, staring at the gelid fat clinging to the ruddy brown beans until the western sky stole all the sunlight away.

Most of the way through his second pack, Louisa Sue came banging in through the house trailer's aluminum door. The only lights inside were the glow of Bester's cigarette and the stuttering green of the microwave's unset clock.

"Daddy?" She sounded scared. She damned well should be scared.

"Dinner's on the table, honey." The cigarettes made his voice croak. Bester swallowed a cough.

"I had a good day at school." She said it like a prayer for peace.

He took a deep breath. It was time to do his duty by his daughter, be the father he had always meant to be. "Just you and that colored boy?"

Louisa Sue sighed. In the dark, she could have been Mavis. Just a woman-shape in his living room. Her words weren't Mavis, though, nor her sharp tone. "He's *African-American*, Daddy, not *colored*, and he has a *name*. Besides, I wasn't with Billy."

"So where were you?"

"School." Even in the shadows, he could see her chin drop, like she always did when she was ashamed of herself. "I got detention for cutting up in ag class. Then I did homework in the library until they kicked me out."

"There's a reason they call it *home*-work," Bester said.

Louisa Sue turned on the kitchenette light, then sat down. Her hair was blue this school year, shaved on the sides like a mental patient. Bester hated the lacy top, hated the parachute pants, hated the loose-tongued workboots, but he'd never been able to control her clothes. He'd burned them, he'd shredded them, he'd given them away, but she always got more. There must be a teen-age underground, supplying clothes to girls with crazy fathers. Despite himself, Bester chuckled at the thought.

Louisa Sue glanced up at him. Her eyes were the same green as Mavis's had been. A small smile quirked her mouth, the first he'd seen in months. "What's funny, Daddy?" she asked, in a voice that reminded him he'd once had a little girl. As she relaxed and settled back in her seat, Louisa Sue's shoulders and chest came up. Bester stared at her. Two dark bumps of her nipples showed.

"Ain't you wearin' no underwear, girl?" he demanded. Bester kicked back his chair and stormed around the table. Louisa Sue shrieked as he grabbed her by the shoulder and yanked her up. Bester tore open her lacy top, the little seed-sized buttons springing away. Louisa Sue's breasts bounced free, the size of oranges. Just like Mavis's, way back when.

One hand on the torn chemise, Bester backhanded his daughter across the cheek. "You been raised better than this." His voice wasn't even angry, just cold. Bester had broken other men's bones when he got that voice on. He pulled back for a real blow, to teach Louisa Sue a lesson she'd never forget, then looked down at his daughter's breasts one more time.

With a blush of shame, his anger was gone.

As soon as Bester let go of the shirt, Louisa Sue ran crying down the short hall to her bedroom. Her door slammed. Her sobs echoed through the thin walls into his conscience, into his heart.

Bester felt hollow. He'd gone too far, run out of choices. He stepped into the kitchenette and took the flour canister down off the fridge. Inside was the old .22 revolver Mavis had used to shoot snakes because she was too scared to kill them with the shovel. Bester pulled out the pistol and wiped the weapon down with a grubby dishcloth. He studied the barrel for a few minutes, played with the action, touched it to his lips. Shame melting to despair, Bester shoved the pistol into the waist pocket of his overalls. Then he went to his daughter's room.

#

The sobs had died to sniffles. It felt stupid, after what he had done, but Bester knocked on Louisa Sue's door anyway.

"Fuck off, Daddy," she shouted after his third try.

"Open up, honey." Bester's right hand fondled the cold metal of the gun in his pocket. "I want to show you how sorry I am."

"No." Louisa Sue began to sob again.

Fighting his anger, Bester leaned his forehead against the door. The thin veneer creaked even under that gentle pressure. Bester's right hand flexed on the grip of the pistol, while his left clenched and unclenched. His eyes stung, peppered with the years of loneliness and the aches of fatherhood. "I ain't gonna ask again, girl," Bester whispered.

There was no answer.

Bester closed his hand on the pistol, cocking it, turned sideways, and slammed his shoulder into Louisa Sue's door. It gave on the first blow, splitting almost down the middle.

As he stepped into Louisa Sue's room, his daughter hurled a ceramic angel at him. It shattered across Bester's forehead like the breaking of heaven.

The last thing he ever heard was Mavis crying.

MR. HEAVEN

Pursued by a rainbow with claws, Eleanor runs through reeds, stumbles on stretch vine, crashes through a stand of wild rose, bleeding from dozens of tiny cuts. Scrambling up a clay bank where Anglos once killed Indians, she slips, bangs her head on an exposed cottonwood root, and falls backward into Plum Creek. As she lies in water up to her ears, the rainbow towers above her like Gabriel at the Annunciation, even to the outspread wings.

"Please don't kill me, Mr. Heaven," she whispers.

"Ha ta bo ho si ko lo," says the angel, which develops noticeable teeth. "Ha sham da ka ba la mesa la." Scales become visible through the rainbow. "Manta lo ho mas si a."

"The gift of tongues!" Eleanor scrambles to her wet knees in prayer. "Our father, who art in Heaven, hallowed be Thy name."

"Ka bo la sham a mas!" thunders the angel, which is now clearly a dragon.

"Thy kingdom come, Thy will be done, on earth as it is in Heaven."

The dragon roars, a massive blast of frustrated energy knocking Eleanor back down into the water. When she blinks away the mud, she is alone, except for a mockingbird that cocks its head at her from a willow branch.

#

Brother Ellison wonders if this is a miracle or psychological instability. He knows that in general that question does not bear close scrutiny.

"After it scourged me, the angel spoke in tongues," Eleanor gasps.

Together they are ankle deep in Plum Creek, looking at the gashes in the mud and the thrown gravel that is evidence of Eleanor's flight from contemplative prayer.

"I am . . . ah . . . honored by your trust, Eleanor," Brother Ellison says. "This should stay within the church, for now. Until we have prayed for guidance."

Eleanor throws her arms around Brother Ellison, leans her head against his chest. "I'm scared, Brother. Scared of the Lord."

"His ways are mysterious, child," says Brother Ellison as he strokes Eleanor's damp hair with his right hand. His left hand wanders lightly down her back.

#

"Must be some gator come a long way up the San Marcos River into Plum Creek," says Deputy Milliken as their cruiser inches through the drive-through lane at Mr. Taco.

"Milky, you don't know shit," says Deputy Strawn. "Gator can't be this far from saltwater."

"Let's go look. If'n we find it, we can shoot it. We'll be he-roes."

Strawn laughs. "Until the Game Warden crawls up our ass. You don't want to pay *that* fine."

"It's endangering public safety." Milliken still has trouble keeping the whine out of his voice, even after his secret visits to the speech therapist up in Austin.

"The only thing endangering public safety around here is Ellie McNulty and her wild-ass tales. Some damned fool thinks the same way you do will be down in Plum Creek shooting at kids drinking beer."

"Might liven things up a bit."

But then it's time for chorizo, eggs and cheese.

#

At the Chisholm Trail Barbecue, the town of Lockhart talks to itself.

"Eleanor McNulty saw a dragon down in Plum Creek."

Tangy red sauce slathers over steaming beef brisket.

"Hah. Ellie sees things everywhere. Remember when she was in high school and saw the unicorn on Center Street? Turned out to be a steer."

Salt sprinkles on butter-raddled carrots.

"It scared her. Honest Injun."

Faded calendars preside on paneled walls like a down-at-the-heels Elk's Hall.

"Everything scares *her*. Probably a blue heron. Was she praying?"

Old folks from the Golden Age Home shuffle through the service line.

"Yep. Straight out the back door of the Fontevrault Bible Church with the tongues of the Lord in her mouth."

Laughter ripples across the room from teenagers perched on vinyl chairs in the corner.

"The Lord moves in mysterious ways His wonders to perform."

#

"Damn," says Manny, "nice to be down here in peace and quiet again." He shoots another beer bottle with his father's .22 pistol. "I'd about had enough of that gator hunt."

Jill, who still won't sleep with Manny even though he's finally got his driver's license, says, "Ellie *McNutty* sure had 'em going."

"Hey, guys!" Otis Lee is ankle deep in the water, over by the sunny side of the bridge abutment. "Lookie here."

Jill leans forward, blowing Manny's careful effort to cop a feel. "What?"

Otis Lee holds up a roughly triangular fish scale the size of a dinner plate. "Found it stuck in the reeds." The scale has a rainbow sheen around the scalloped edge, while the narrow end is dark as night.

The scale doesn't break when Otis Lee smashes it against the concrete of the bridge, but it bursts into hundreds of pretty shards when Manny shoots it.

#

In her room in the attic of her grandmother's house, Eleanor cries into her pillow most of the time, and prays when she isn't crying. "Next time," she tells the summer sky lurking outside her window, "I swear I'll do whatever Mr. Heaven wants."

THE GOAT CUTTER

The Devil lives in Houston by the ship channel in a high-rise apartment fifty-seven stories up. They say he's got cowhide sofas and a pinball machine and a telescope in there that can see past the oil refineries and across Pasadena all the way to the Pope in Rome and on to where them Arabs pray to that big black stone.

He can see anyone anywhere from his place in the Houston sky, and he can see inside their hearts.

But I know it's all a lie. Except about the hearts, of course. Cause I know the Devil lives in an old school bus in the woods outside of Dale, Texas. He don't need no telescope to see inside your heart, on account of he's already there.

This I know.

#

Central Texas gets mighty hot come summer. The air rolls in heavy off the Gulf, carries itself over two hundred miles of cow shit and sorghum fields and settles heavy on all our heads. The katydids buzz in the woods like electric fans with bad bearings, and even the skeeters get too tired to bite most days. You can smell the dry coming off the Johnson grass and out of the bar ditches.

Me and my best friend Pootie, we liked to run through the woods, climbing bob wire and following pipelines. Trees is smaller there, easier to slip between. You gotta watch out in deer season, though. Idiots come out from Austin or San Antone to their leases, get blind drunk and shoot every blessed thing that moves. Rest of the time, there's nothing but you and them turkey vultures. Course, you can't steal beer coolers from turkey vultures.

The Devil, he gets on pretty good with them turkey vultures.

So me and Pootie was running the woods one afternoon somewhere in the middle of summer. We was out of school, waiting to be sopho-mores in the fall, fixing to amount to something. Pootie was bigger than me, but I already got tongue off Martha Dempsey. Just a week or so ago back of the church hall, I even scored a little titty squeeze inside her shirt. It was over her bra, but that counts for something. I knew I was coming up good.

Pootie swears he saw Rachel MacIntire's nipples, but she's his cousin. I reckoned he just peeked through the bathroom window of his aunt's trailer house, which ain't no different from me watching Momma get out of the shower. It don't count. If there was anything to it, he'd a sucked on 'em, and I'd of never heard the end of *that*. Course I wouldn't say no to my cousin Linda if she offered to show me a little something in the shower.

Yeah, that year we was big boys, the summer was hot, and we was always hungry and horny.

Then we met the Devil.

#

Me and Pootie crossed the bob wire fence near the old bus wallow on county road 61, where they finally built that little bridge over the draw. Doug Bob Aaronson had that place along the south side of 61, spent his time roasting goats, drinking tequila and shooting people's dogs.

Doug Bob was okay, if you didn't bring a dog. Three years back, once we turned ten, he let me and Pootie drink his beer with him. He liked to liquor up, strip down to his underwear and get his ass real warm from the fire in his smoker. We was just a guy and two kids in their shorts drinking in the woods. I'm pretty sure Momma and Uncle Reuben would of had hard words, so I never told.

We kind of hoped now that we was going to be sophomores, he'd crack some of that *Sauza Conmemorativo Anejo* for us.

Doug Bob's place was all grown over, wild rose and stretch vine and beggar's lice everywhere, and every spring a huge-ass wisteria wrapped his old cedar house with lavender flowers and thin whips of wood. There was trees all around in the brush, mesquite and hackberry and live-oak and juniper and a few twisty old pecans. Doug Bob knew all the plants and trees, and taught 'em to us sometimes when he was less than half drunk. He kept chickens around the place and a mangy duck that waddled away funny whenever he got to looking at it.

We come crashing through the woods one day that summer, hot, hungry, horny and full of fight. Pootie'd told me about Rachel's nipples, how they was set in big pink circles and stuck out like little red thumbs. I told him I'd seen that picture in *Hustler* same as him. If'n he was gonna lie, lie from a magazine I hadn't stole us from the Triple E Grocery.

Doug Bob's cedar house was bigger than three doublewides. It set at the back of a little clearing by the creek that ran down from the bus wallow. He lived there, fifty feet from a rusted old school bus that he wouldn't never set foot inside. Only time I asked him about that bus, he cracked me upside the head so hard I saw double for days and had to tell Uncle Reuben I fell off my bike.

That would of been a better lie if I'd of recollected that my bike'd been stolen three weeks gone. Uncle Reuben didn't beat me much worse than normal, and we prayed extra long over the Bible that night for forgiveness.

Doug Bob was pretty nice. He about never hit me, and he kept his underpants on when I was around.

#

That old smoker was laid over sidewise on the ground, where it didn't belong. Generally, Doug Bob kept better care of it than anything except an open bottle of tequila. He had cut the smoker from a gigantic water heater, so big me and Pootie could of slept in it. Actually, we did a couple of times, but you can't never get ash out of your hair after.

And Pootie snored worse than Uncle Reuben.

Doug Bob roasted his goats in that smoker, and he was mighty particular about his goats. He always killed his goats hisself. They didn't usually belong to him, but he did his own killing. Said it made him a better man. I thought it mostly made him a better mess. The meat plant over in Lockhart could of done twice the job in half the time, with no bath in the creek afterward.

Course, when you're sweaty and hot and full of piss and vinegar, there's nothing like a splash around down in the creek with some beer and one of them big cakes of smelly purple horse soap me and Pootie stole out of barns for Doug Bob. Getting rubbed down with that stuff kind of stings, but it's a good sting.

Times like that, I knew Doug Bob liked me just for myself. We'd all smile and laugh and horse around and get drunk. Nobody got hit, nobody got hurt, everybody went home happy.

#

Doug Bob always had one of these goats, and it was always a buck. Sometimes a white Saanen, or maybe a creamy La Mancha or a brown Nubian looked like a chubby deer with them barred goat eyes staring straight into your heart. They was always clean, no socks nor blazes nor points, just one color all over. Doug Bob called them *unblemished*.

And Doug Bob always killed these goats on the north side of the smoker. He had laid some rocks down there, to make a clear spot for when it was muddy from winter rain or whatever. He'd cut their throats with his jagged knife that was older than sin, and sprinkle the blood all around the smoker.

He never let me touch that knife.

#

Doug Bob, he had this old gray knife without no handle, just rags wrapped up around the end. The blade had a funny shape like it got beat up inside a thresher or something, same as happened to Momma's sister Maizie the year I was born. Her face had that funny shape until Uncle Reuben found her hanging in the pole barn one morning with her dress up over her head.

They puttied her up for the viewing at the funeral home, but I recall Aunt Maizie best with those big dents in her cheek and jaw and the one brown eye gone all white like milk in coffee.

Doug Bob's knife, that I always thought of as Maizie's knife, it was kind of wompered and shaped all wrong, like a corn leaf the bugs been at. He'd take that knife and saw the head right off his goat.

I never could figure how Doug Bob kept that edge on.

He'd flay that goat, and strip some fatback off the inside of the hide, and put the head and the fat right on the smoker where the fire was going, wet chips of mesquite over a good hot bed of coals.

Then he'd drag the carcass down to creek, to our swimming hole, and sometimes me and Pootie could help with this part. We'd wash out the gut sack and clean off the heart and lungs and liver. Doug Bob always scrubbed the legs specially well with that purple horse soap. We'd generally get a good lot of blood in the water. If it hadn't rained in a while, like most summers, the water'd be sticky for hours afterward.

Doug Bob would take the carcass and the sweetbreads — that's what he called the guts, sweetbreads. I figured they looked more like spongy purple and red bruises than bread, kind of like dog food fresh outta the can. And there wasn't nothing sweet about them.

Sweetbreads taste better than dog food, though. We ate dog food in the winter sometimes, ate it cold if Uncle Reuben didn't have work and Momma'd been lazy. That was when I most missed my summers in the woods with Pootie, calling in on Doug Bob.

Doug Bob would drag these goat parts back up to the smoker, where he'd take the head and the fat off the fire. He'd always give me and Pootie some of that fat, to keep us away from the head meat, I guess. Doug Bob would put the carcass and the sweetbreads on the fire and spit his high-proof tequila all over them. If they didn't catch straight away from that, he'd light 'em with a bic.

We'd watch them burn, quiet and respectful like church on account of that's what Doug Bob believed. He always said God told him to keep things orderly, somewhere in the beginning of Leviticus.

Then he'd close the lid and let the meat cook. He didn't never clean up the blood around the smoker, although he would catch some to write Bible verses on the sides of that old school bus with.

#

The Devil lives in San Francisco in a big apartment on Telegraph Hill. Way up there with all that brass and them potted ferns and naked women with leashes on, he's got a telescope that can see across the bay, even in the fog. They say he can see all the way to China and Asia, with little brown people and big red demon gods, and stare inside their hearts.

The Devil, he can see inside everybody's heart, just about.

It's a lie, except that part about the hearts. There's only one place in God's wide world where the Devil can't see.

#

Me and Pootie, we found that smoker laying over on its side, which we ain't never seen. There was a broken tequila bottle next to it, which ain't much like Doug Bob neither.

Well, we commenced to running back and forth, calling out "Doug Bob!" and "Mr. Aaronson!" and stuff. That was dumb cause if he was around and listening, he'd of heard us giggling and arguing by the time we'd crossed his fence line.

I guess we both knew that, cause pretty quick we fell quiet and starting looking around. I felt like I was on TV or something, and there was a bad thing fixing to happen next. Them saloon doors were flapping in my mind and I started wishing mightily for a commercial.

#

That old bus of Doug Bob's, it was a long bus, like them revival preachers use to bring their people into town. I always thought going to Glory when you died meant getting on one of them buses painted white and gold, with Bible verses on the side and a choir clapping and singing in the back and some guy in a powder blue suit and hair like a raccoon pelt kissing you on the cheek and slapping you on the forehead.

Well, I been kissed more than I want to, and I don't know nobody with a suit, no matter the color, and there ain't no choir ever going to sing me to my rest now, except if maybe they're playing bob wire harps and beating time on burnt skulls. But Doug Bob's bus, it sat there flat on the dirt with the wiry bones of tires wrapped over dented black hubs grown with morning glory, all yellow with the rusted old metal showing through, with the windows painted black from the inside and crossed over with duct tape. It had a little vestibule Doug Bob'd built over the double doors out of wood from an old church in Rosanky. The entrance to that vestibule was crossed over with duct tape just like the windows. It was bus number seven, whatever place it had come from.

And bus number seven was covered with them Bible verses written in goat's blood, over and over each other to where there was just red-brown smears on the cracked windshield and across the hood and down the sides, scrambled scribbling that looked like Aunt Maizie's drool on the lunch table at Wal-Mart. And they made about as much sense.

I even seen Doug Bob on the roof of that bus a few times, smearing bloody words with his fingers like a message to the turkey vultures, or maybe all the way to God above looking down from His air-conditioned heaven.

So I figured, the smoker's tipped, the tequila's broke, and here's my long bus bound for glory with Bible verses on the side, and the only choir is the katydids buzzing in the trees and me and Pootie breathing hard. I saw the door of the wooden vestibule on the bus, that Doug Bob never would touch, was busted open, like it had been kicked out from the inside. The duct tape just flapped loose from the door frame.

I stared all around that bus, and there was a new verse on the side, right under the driver's window. It was painted fresh, still shiny and red. It said, "Of the tribe of Reuben were sealed twelve thousand."

"Pootie."

"Huh?" He was gasping pretty hard. I couldn't take my eyes off the bus, which looked as if it was gonna rise up from the dirt and rumble down the road to salvation any moment, but I knew Pootie had that wild look where his eyes get almost all white and his nose starts to bleed. I could tell from his breathing.

Smelled like he wet his pants, too.

"Pootie," I said again, "there ain't no fire, and there ain't no fresh goat been killed. Where'd the blood come from for that there Bible verse?"

"Reckon he talking 'bout your Uncle?" Pootie's voice was duller than Momma at Christmas.

Pootie was an idiot. Uncle Reuben never had no twelve thousand in his life. If he ever did, he'd of gone to Mexico and to hell with me and Momma. "Pootie," I tried again, "where'd the blood come from?"

I knew, but I didn't want to be the one to say it.

Pootie panted for a little while longer. I finally tore my eyes off that old bus, which was shimmering like summer heat, to see Pootie bent over with his hands on his knees and his head hanging down. "It ain't his handwritin' neither," Pootie sobbed.

We both knew Doug Bob was dead.

#

Something was splashing around down by the creek. "Aw, shit," I said. "Doug Bob was—is—our friend. We gotta go look."

It ain't but a few steps to the bank. We could see a man down there, bending over with his bare ass toward us. He was washing something big and pale. It weren't no goat.

Me and Pootie, we stopped at the top of the bank, and the stranger stood up and turned around. I about shit my pants.

He had muscles like a movie star, and a gold tan all the way down,

64

like he'd never wore clothes. The hair on his chest and his short-and-curlies was blonde, and he was hung good. What near to made me puke was that angel's body had a goat head. Only it weren't no goat head you ever saw in your life.

It was like a big heavy ram's head, except it had *antlers* coming up off the top, a twelve point spread off a prize buck, and baby's eyes—big, blue and round in the middle. Not goat's eyes at all. That fur kind of tapered off into golden skin at the neck.

And those blue eyes blazed at me like ice on fire.

The tall, golden thing pointed to a body in the creek. He'd been washing the legs with purple soap. "Help me with this. I think you know how it needs to be done." His voice was windy and creaky, like he hadn't talked to no one for a real long time.

The body was Doug Bob, with his big gut and saggy butt, and a bloody stump of a neck.

"You son of a bitch!" I ran down the bank, screaming and swinging my arms for the biggest punch I could throw. I don't know, maybe I tripped over a root or stumbled at the water's edge, but that golden thing moved like summer lightning just as I slipped off my balance.

Last thing I saw was the butt end of Doug Bob's ragged old knife coming at me in his fist. I heard Pootie crying my name when my head went all red and painful.

#

The Devil lives in your neighborhood, yours and mine. He lives in every house in every town, and he has a telescope that looks out the bathroom mirror and up from the drains in the kitchen and out of the still water at the bottom of the toilet bowl. He can see inside of everyone's heart through their eyes and down their mouth and up their asshole.

It's true, I know it is.

The hope I hold secret deep inside my heart is that there's one place on God's green earth the Devil can't see.

\#

I was naked, my dick curled small and sticky to my thigh like it does after I've been looking through the bathroom window. A tight little trail of cum itched my skin. My ass was on dirt, and I could feel ants crawling up the crack. I opened my mouth to say, "Fine," and a fly buzzed out from the inside. There was another one in the left side of my nose that seemed ready to stay a spell.

I didn't really want to open my eyes. I knew where I was. My back was against hot metal. It felt sticky. I was leaning against Doug Bob's bus and part of that new Bible verse about Uncle Reuben under the driver's window had run and got Doug Bob's heart blood all down my back. I could smell mesquite smoke, cooked meat, shit, blood, and the old oily metal of the bus.

But in all my senses, in the feel of the rusted metal, in the warmth of the ground, in the stickiness of the blood, in the sting of the ant bites, in the touch of the fly crawling around inside my nose, in the stink of Doug Bob's rotten little yard, there was something missing. It was an absence, a space, like when you get a tooth busted out in a fight, and notice it for not being there.

I was surrounded by absence, cold in the summer heat. My heart felt real slow. I still didn't want to open my eyes.

"You know," said that windy, creaky voice, sounding even more hollow and thin than before, "if they would just repent of their murders, their sorceries, their fornication, and their thefts, this would be a lot harder."

The voice was sticky, like the blood on my back, and cold, coming from the middle of whatever was missing around me. I opened my eyes and squinted into the afternoon sun.

Doug Bob's face smiled at me. Leastwise it tried to. Up close I could tell a whole lot of it was burnt off, with griddle marks where his head had lain a while on the smoker. Blackened bone showed through across the cheeks. Doug Bob's head was duct taped to the neck of that glorious, golden body, greasy black hair falling down those perfect shoulders. The head kept trying to lop over as he moved, like it was stuck on all wompered. His face was puffy and burnt up, weirder than Doug Bob mostly ever looked.

The smoker must of been working again.

#

The golden thing with Doug Bob's head had Pootie spread out naked next to the smoker. I couldn't tell if he was dead, but sure he wasn't moving. Doug Bob's legs hung over the side of the smoker, right where he'd always put the goat legs. Maizie's crazy knife was in that golden right hand, hanging loose like Uncle Reuben holds his when he's fixing to fight someone.

"I don't understand . . . " I tried to talk, but burped up a little bit of vomit and another fly to finish my sentence. The inside of my nose stung with the smell, and the fly in there didn't seem to like it much neither. "You stole Doug Bob's head."

"You see, my son, I have been set free from my confinement. My time is at hand." Doug Bob's face wrinkled into a smile, as some of his burnt lip scaled away. I wondered how much of Doug Bob was still down in the creek. "But even I can not walk the streets with my proud horns."

His voice got sweeter, stronger, as he talked. I stared up at him, blinking in the sunlight.

"Rise up and join me. We have much work to do, preparations for my triumph. As the first to bow to my glory you shall rank high among my new disciples, and gain your innermost desire."

Uncle Reuben taught me long ago how this sweet bullshit always ends. The old Doug Bob liked me. Maybe even loved me a little. He was always kind to me, which this golden Doug Bob ain't never gonna be.

It must be nice to be loved a lot.

I staggered to my feet, farting ants, using the ridges in the sheet metal of the bus for support. It was hot as hell, and even the katydids had gone quiet. Except for the turkey vultures circling low over me, I felt like I was alone in a giant dirt coffin with a huge blue lid over my head. I felt expanded, swollen in the heat like a dead coyote by the side of the road.

The thing wearing Doug Bob's head narrowed his eyes at me. There was a faint crinkling sound as the lids creased and broke.

"Get over here, *now*." His voice had the menace of a Sunday morning twister headed for a church, the power of a wall of water in the arroyo where kids played.

I walked toward the Devil, feet stepping without my effort.

#

There's a place I can go, inside, when Uncle Reuben's pushing into me, or he's using the metal end of the belt, or Momma's screaming through the thin walls of our trailer the way he can make her do. It's like ice cream without the cone, like cotton candy without the stick. It's like how I imagine Rachel MacIntire's nipples, sweet and total, like my eyes and heart are in my lips and the world has gone dark around me.

It's the place where I love myself, deep inside my heart.

I went there and listened to the little shuffling of my pulse in my ears.

My feet walked on without me, but I couldn't tell.

#

Maizie's knife spoke to me. The Devil must of put it in my hand.

"We come again to Moriah," it whispered in my heart. It had a voice like its metal blade, cold from the ground and old as time.

"What do you want?" I asked. I must of spoke out loud, because Doug Bob's burned mouth was twisting in screaming rage as he stabbed his golden finger down toward Pootie, naked at my feet next to the smoker. All I could hear was my pulse, and the voice of the knife.

Deep inside my heart, the knife whispered again. "Do not lay a hand on the boy."

The golden voice from Doug Bob's face was distant thunder in my ears. I felt his irritation, rage, frustration building where I had felt that cold absence.

I tried again. "I don't understand."

Doug Bob's head bounced up and down, the duct tape coming loose. I saw pink ropy strings working to bind the burned head to his golden neck. He cocked back a fist, fixing to strike me a hard blow.

I felt the knife straining across the years toward me. "You have a choice. The Enemy promises anything and everything for your help. I can offer you nothing but the hope of an orderly world. You choose what happens now, and after."

I reckoned the Devil would run the world about like Uncle Reuben might. Doug Bob was already dead, and Pootie was next, and there wasn't nobody else like them in my life, no matter what the Devil promised. I figured there was enough hurt to go around already and I knew how to take it into me.

Another one of Uncle Reuben's lessons.

"Where you want this killing done?" I asked.

The golden thunder in my ears paused for a moment, the tide of rage lapped back from the empty place where Doug Bob wasn't. The fist dropped down.

"Right here, right now," whispered the knife. "Or it will be too late. Seven is being opened."

I stepped out of my inside place to find my eyes still open and Doug Bob's blackened face inches from my nose. His teeth were burnt and cracked, and his breath reeked of flies and red meat. I smiled, opened my mouth to speak, but instead of words I swung Maizie's knife right through the duct tape at the throat of Doug Bob's head.

He looked surprised.

Doug Bob's head flew off, bounced into the bushes. The golden body swayed, still on its two feet. I looked down at Pootie, the old knife cold in my hands.

Then I heard buzzing, like thunder made of wires.

#

I don't know if you ever ate a fly, accidental or not. They go down fighting, kind of tickle the throat, you get a funny feeling for a second, and then it's all gone. Not very filling, neither.

69

These flies came pouring out of the ragged neck of that golden body. They were big, the size of horseflies. All at once they were everywhere, and they came right at me. They came pushing at my eyes and my nose and my ears and flying right into my mouth, crawling down my throat. It was like stuffing yourself with raisins till you choke, except these raisins crawled and buzzed and bit at me.

The worst was they got all over me, crowding into my butt crack and pushing on my asshole and wrapping around my balls like Uncle Reuben's fingers right before he squeezed tight. My skin rippled, as if them flies crawled through my flesh.

I jumped around, screaming and slapping at myself. My gut heaved, but my throat was full of flies and it all met in a knot at the back of my mouth. I rolled to the ground, choking on the rippling mess I couldn't spit out nor swallow back down. Through the flies I saw Doug Bob's golden body falling in on itself, like a balloon that's been popped. Then the choking took me off.

#

I lied about the telescope. I don't need one.

Right after, while I was still mostly myself, I sent Pootie away with that old knife to find one of Doug Bob's kin. They needed that knife, to make their sacrifices that would keep me shut away. I made Pootie seal me inside the bus with Doug Bob's duct tape before he left.

The bus is hot and dark, but I don't really mind. There's just me and the flies and a hot metal floor with rubber mats and huge stacks of old Bibles and hymnals that make it hard for me to move around.

It's okay, though, because I can watch the whole world from in here.

I hate the flies, but they're the only company I can keep. The taste grows on me.

I know Pootie must of found someone to give that old knife to. I try the doors sometimes, but they hold firm. Somewhere one of Doug Bob's brothers or uncles or cousins cuts goats the old way. Someday I'll find him. I can see every heart except one, but there are too many to easily tell one from another.

There's only one place under God's golden sun the Devil can't see into, and that's his own heart.

#

I still have my quiet place. That's where I hold my hope, and that's where I go when I get too close to the goat cutter.

GODS

CHRISTMAS SEASON

Every year come Friday after Thanksgiving, Pawpaw gets to cleaning his shotgun. "Millie Ann," he always tells me, "This is gonna be our best Christmas ever." What he means is we'll eat Christmas sausage for months. That's good. Daddy don't earn much, and we won't take government handouts, so we don't get food stamps or nothing.

Pawpaw is Ma's Daddy. On account of Ma dying when I was four and Daddy's work oil rigging keeping him away so much, Pawpaw pretty much raises me himself.

Pawpaw sits there singing, "On Comet, on Cupid, on Donder and Blitzen," while he cleans the barrel of his old ten gauge. He likes carols about reindeer and Santa's sleigh.

"Up on the housetop, click, click, click," as he loads the shotgun shells. Pawpaw smiles at me. "Next year Millie Ann, when you are thirteen, you can help me with the reloads."

"Thank you, Pawpaw." This seems like a good time to ask. "Can I come tonight? I hate staying with Aunt Gemma. Her trailer smells like cat pee and her cookies are always stale."

Pawpaw smacks his lips as he stares at me. That means he's thinking. "I reckon you're old enough this year, girl."

"Goodie!" Pawpaw doesn't think I'm a little kid any more. I grin so hard my teeth feel like to fall out.

#

It's real early Saturday morning, so early it's almost still Friday. Our hunting blind is at the edge of some trees above a long, sloping field with more trees at the bottom. There's a few other blinds around. When we got here those folks made a big fuss over my first Christmas season. That was nice, and it made me feel important. Now it's so cold my hands ache. Pawpaw drinks coffee to keep warm, but I can't have none 'cause it'll make me short. After a while, Pawpaw taps his watch. "Coming up on moonrise." He shoulders his ten gauge.

As the world lights up under the silver moon, a weird barking echoes from the woods. I see a red light drift into the sky, like ember off a bonfire. Another one winks on, then two more. Suddenly it's like fireflies on a summer evening, only they're big and red, like from a roman candle. A gun fires. One of the lights drops to the ground with a little shriek, sputtering as it falls. The swarm darts toward us. Pawpaw begins to fire too, blazing away and yelling about Viet Cong.

Even with my fingers in my ears, the shotgun is so loud it's scary. I keep looking, though. I don't want to miss any of it. All around, folks are shooting, everybody cutting loose to catch the swarm before it rises too high. One by one, they fall crying like wounded angels from the moonlit sky.

#

I weep over a small one. Up close, they're just tiny deer, no bigger than a housecat. Their little noses stop glowing a few minutes after they're dead, looking like cherries set out too long. "It's Rudolph," I say through sniffles. I don't want to cry, because Pawpaw might decide I was a baby after all.

Pawpaw dumps bodies in the back of the pick-up. What with all the shooting, there's plenty here for everybody. "Buck up, Millie Ann. You always knew where Christmas sausage came from."

"Yeah." I wipe my nose on my sleeve. "It just seemed to hurt them so much."

Pawpaw sighs. "They breed like crazy, hatch out same as locusts. We kill most of them now, leave just enough to make it north for mating season without wrecking fields and farms along the way. They get a lot bigger up there in the Arctic, come back to breed and start things all over again."

I think about all those other farmers we are helping. I swallow my tears. "We got to eat something, don't we?"

"That's right." Pawpaw smiles. "I love Christmas season."

TWILIGHT OF THE ODD

Today is Friday [the 13th].

This is the story of the Egg Tree at the heart of the world and how it helped me save us all from Thimble Winter. I am telling how it happened to this tape recorder for Mister Hale the County Attorney on account of Judge Nagle told me to or else I had to go to jail or the State Home, whichever. Judge Nagle, she says Doris the clerk of the court will write this tape out for me in a statement.

My name is Vidor Ezer. I live in Ranger Rock, Texas, which is the county seat of Middleyard County. I don't want to tell this story but I don't want to go to jail neither. I don't always talk so good, so I am sorry if it takes a long time to read this.

Once when I was a boy a nice lady from the state read me some stories from a picture book. I don't much remember the book no more, but there was an Egg Tree what grew under the ground in the cellar of the world down in its big stone heart. Well, we got that Egg Tree right here in Ranger Rock.

Nana King, she is my mama's mama. She says my Daddy's people should have stayed in Norway with all the other dumb oxes. She hates him. A lot of people do. My Daddy's name is Wooden Ezer, on account of his Daddy wanted all his boys to grow up right powerful. Uncle Iron is in the federal pen in Kansas. Uncle Strong got hisself killed in the Army. Daddy says Strong was shooting Commies, like John Wayne, but

78

Hines read the letter and one time when he was drunk he told me Strong got shot by police outside a bar in Seoul.

Nana King lets us live in one of her rent houses down in the bottomland by Rainbow Crick. She won't give us no money, so we mostly don't have no lights or propane, but at least we got a roof over our heads like Daddy says. Me and Daddy live there with my brother Fore. Fore's kind of weird.

Fred Ayer and Hines Dell live there too. We mostly have enough to eat.

Lookie Glass and Sparky Surtees and the Hardison brothers down in Must Hill, they call us the Odd. I guess that makes our house the Odd House. The cellar of the Odd House has a dirt floor, and that's where the roots of the Egg Tree come in.

Sometimes at night I go down there in the dark when Daddy and Fore and Fred and Hines are drinking and listen to the roots. They whisper to me and tell important secrets. Sometimes I find an egg down there. I most always eat the eggs, and their secrets become a part of me for a little while.

#

Today is Monday [the 16th].

Them big Red Cross trucks left this morning. Almost everybody is back in their homes now. Sheriff Fader told me I was supposed to say in my statement that I ain't living with Daddy and them in the Odd house no more. Sheriff Fader and Missus Sheriff Fader are letting me stay in their spare room. This is on account of the nearest State Home is in Kerrville and Judge Nagle figures I am better off here in Ranger Rock with people who know me.

So here is my story. One day in February it snowed. Ranger Rock don't get much snow never. It don't get much rain never either. I only seen it snow twice since I can remember as a little kid. It snowed on Friday, like the whole sky was paint flaking off a school wall. You think snow is soft, but for real it's hard and prickly. It gets in your hair and your shirt and on your feet and makes you cold like an ice cube. I hate it.

"Watch out for the Hardison Brothers," said the Egg Tree. I was hiding in the cellar from the snow. I was listening to its roots.

I said, "What are they going to do?"

"They will put the world in darkness," said the Egg Tree. It said it more fancy, but I can't remember the big words so good. But I remember that it said this: "You must stop them."

So I went outside to look. The snow it was cold. I went to the Sheriff's Station to tell Sheriff Fader to watch out for the Hardison Brothers but he was gone to Austin for a state Sheriffs' meeting. Back then I didn't get along with his main deputy Feist, so I went along my own way. I tried to figure how the Hardison Brothers was going to turn out the lights.

It snowed for three days. On Sunday it stopped for a while, and lots of the snow become water everywhere, but it started snowing again on Monday for three more days. Daddy and Fore got in a big fight. Fore put on his special gloves that Uncle Strong sent him from Korea and got his hammer and he whipped Daddy's ass. So Hines and Fred got on Fore and stuffed snow down his shirt and hurt him until Fore said he was sorry. I knew he didn't mean it, though. Then Hines hid away the hammer.

#

Now it is Tuesday the 17th.

Sheriff Fader says I got to say the dates for my statement. I am trying on account of I don't want to go to jail. Plus Mrs. Sheriff is nice to make my favorite foods for dinner so I want Sheriff to be proud of me.

That Wednesday night it stopped snowing again. There was about knee high snow with cold water running away from it in the street. It was freak weather, they said on our radio station. That is KYGG 790 on my AM dial. I listen sometimes when I can get a battery for my little radio, which I had this time when it snowed.

That night we all went out to celebrate the snow and hunt for omens. Daddy and Fore and Hines and Fred and Me, we was all dressed in our special clothes. Daddy had his raven mask on and Fore had his Viking helmet. It's really a purple football helmet with cow horns duct taped on. Hines wore his band uniform, pushing his shopping cart full of trumpets and bugles. Fred had on his sun suit, which is what he calls it when he is naked in his skin. Me, I'm always at the end of the line on account of being the youngest even though I'm bigger than Fred. I just wore my blue jeans and my bowling shirt from the thrift store, but I had a new egg from the Egg Tree in my pocket in case I needed to be smart sudden like.

We all went out in the snow. We was in our parade, like we do when things are special. Lookie and them always mess with us, but we know what we know over at the Odd House.

We was marching toward the Santa Fe railroad grade crossing when I heard a big whump. It sounded like the time Porky Smutts at the lumberyard wrecked the tallboy forklift and dropped four hundred pounds of plywood on our town fire truck. All the lights went out, which I could tell on account of it was night. The snow was done, but the sky was all clouds, and there weren't no moon or stars. All we could see was a fire on the other side of the tracks, where the big power lines come into town.

I knew it was the Hardison Brothers putting the world into darkness like the Egg Tree had said.

"That's what we came for," said Daddy. Fore and Hines and Fred began hooting and hollering. We all commenced to running when I heard that big howl.

That was Fentress, Lookie Glass's big giant dog. I once heard Sheriff Fader call it the hound of the basketballs on account of it was as big as Charles Barkley the NBA star. Fentress was like to the size of a horse. Fentress had got loose from Gleap Near which is what they called his pen at the end of town. That dog would chew down the moon if it could, and I knew there was going to be trouble.

The railroad tracks, they run alongside Rainbow Crick that runs through Ranger Rock. The snow was all over town, and the crick was running high. There's a dam outside the town which is our reserve war for the drought every summer. The radio kept saying there was too much water behind the dam from the weather.

We was running through the snow next to the railroad tracks and I could hear banging noises from downtown where Fentress was chewing on car tires until they exploded. I looked down and the water was getting real big real fast.

"Daddy," I said. "Look at the water."

Daddy looked down and stopped so Fore ran into him. Hines ran his cart into Fore, but Fred didn't hit Hines. I figured his willie must be freezing fit to fall off but Fred just kept talking on real quiet about sun and light.

Excuse me. Sheriff Fader says I got to give back the tape recorder now.

#

Thursday the 19th

I'm sorry I missed a day. The State of Texas sent some people to look at our town. They came in a hello chopper. They're supposed to make us a disaster area. Plus some people from Texas A&M wanted to look at Fentress. They wanted to talk to me too.

After they bothered me for a while Sheriff Fader run them off and promised to send them my statement when I am done. So hi to you professors and I'm sorry I bit the pretty lady's hand.

And here is more of my story. There was about two feet of snow on the ground. The power station was on fire on account of Skoal and Haddie Hardison had set off some dynamite over there. Fentress was loose in town biting the tires off cars. Then the dam broke open and flooded down Rainbow Crick.

It was spilling the banks of Rainbow Crick and getting up toward the feedlot and the lumberyard over by the tracks. I knew the Odd House would get flooded and a lot of other places. By then I guess Daddy figured the power station could take care of itself. Our parade turned back to help the town.

The egg in my pocket started to bounce around. I didn't know what that meant. The Egg Tree had never done that to me before. The egg tugged inside my pocket, pulling me toward the Sheriff's Station. I knew Lookie Glass and Jaime Norte were in the jail there along with two Mexican wrestlers busted for dealing from a traveling show. I have their names on a poster I saved in my pocket.

Wait a minute.

OK. Los Hermanos Gigantescos; Escarcha and Fuego. I will give this poster to Doris the clerk so she can write the names good.

"Daddy," I said. "We got to go down to the jail."

Daddy didn't listen to me. He and the others were singing "Onward Christian Soldiers" real loud, except Hines was blowing on a bugle while he pushed his shopping cart.

I run down to the jail then by myself. The Egg Tree's egg was bouncing in my pocket like a super ball from the Wal-Mart. It pulled against the cloth of my blue jeans.

Lamar Street where the Sheriff's Station is was flooded from the dam breaking. The water had rose above my knees with dirty snow and chunks of ice floating in it. There was black things like burned up bear claws from the bakery that was pieces of car tire. I saw Deputy Feist had opened up the doors and was letting the drunks out to climb on the roof where he had a ladder.

The egg in my pocket commenced to jouncing real hard and then Lookie Glass and Jaime Norte come out of the jail while Deputy Feist was helping Margie Plunkett onto the ladder. Feist he didn't see them and frowned at me just when Jaime cold-cocked him with a desk lamp from behind.

Even though he did not like me I run over and pulled Feist out of the water where he fell on account of I was afraid he was going to drown while Margie stood on the ladder and screamed about spiders and kept spitting at me.

The egg bounced so hard I pulled it out of my pocket. . . . It was all warm and slippery but somehow I didn't drop it. The Egg Tree helps me a lot, so I figured it might help the Deputy. So I put it on the bloody patch on the back of Feist's head and he stopped bleeding so I took him inside and laid him on a desk where there was less water on account of the two steps up to the floor.

#

Friday the 20th.

After he read what Doris wrote from my tape records Sheriff Fader said if I was going to lie not to do it in this statement. Judge Nagle said I was to tell the truth, all of the truth and nothing else.

I didn't lie I swear about the egg and Deputy Feist. His head was all wompered and bloody where Jaime cold cocked him and the egg helped. I ain't not going to tell no more today on account of Sheriff Fader saying I'm a liar.

#

Monday [the 23rd].

Mrs. Sheriff Fader says I am not a liar. She is a nurse practice sinner at the clinic and after they argued about me for a while she made Deputy Feist get his head examined. Elmo Sinclair that runs the lab there made a X-ray picture of Deputy Feist's head and they said, "Here look. There is evidence of bone nits in here."

They have been arguing about medical records and stuff but I know it was the Egg Tree that saved Deputy Feist and Mrs. Sheriff Fader knows it was the Egg Tree but says she doesn't know how and Sheriff knows it too but he won't admit it was the Egg Tree on account of Judge Nagle says I am of diminished capacity. I wrote that down, like the evidence of the bone nits nitting together. I can be pretty clever.

[laughter]

And Sheriff thinks this means I am crazy which he won't say neither but the Egg Tree saved Deputy Feist all the same no matter what.

Excuse me because I have to read back in the copy of my statement Doris the clerk made and remember where I stopped.

Okay. I went back outside and Lookie Glass had lit out for the high cotton. Except he came back later but I am getting ahead of myself. Jaime and the Mexican wrestlers stole Judge Nagle's bass boat from her driveway, which she lives only a block and half from the Sheriff's station on Pecan Street. They was buzzing down Lamar Street whooping and hollering and throwing stuff through some of the windows of the stores and stuff.

I figured Deputy Feist was going to be okay so I followed the boat. The egg it had stopped jumping around so the Egg Tree must have been okay with me helping the Deputy. Maybe it didn't want no one to die.

It was still real dark and the water was everywhere. I was afraid of Fentress but the dog must of gone uphill toward the main square to get away from the flood. Of course the bass boat got away from me fast so I wandered around in the dark for a while looking for Daddy and Fore and Fred and Hines. After a while my legs started cramping real bad from the cold in the water and I had to head up hill too.

I wondered where everyone was. It is not every day that the town floods but it was late at night too. I began singing my favorite hymn from church which Mrs. Sheriff Fader hates it when I sing at her house. Which it is, "Drop Kick Me Jesus Through the Goal Posts of Life."

Singing made me feel warmer but my cramps were bad until I got up the hill where I found a lot of people and I was soon to be sorry I did.

#

Tuesday [the] 24th.

Doris says I forgot to say the date again yesterday. This morning a man came from San Antonio. He was a Catholic man in a black dress on account of Deputy Feist is Catholic and Missus Deputy Feist told her priest I saved his life and it was a miracle.

Sheriff Fader let the Catholic man read my statement after he talked with Judge Nagle. Missus Deputy Feist says I need my friends although I am no longer maybe going to be charged with a salting of the deputy on account of my this-here testimony.

And the Catholic man said, "I will need a copy of the X-rays and your police reports." And he asked for other things. He asked me about the Egg Tree and said, "The cross of Jesus is sometimes called a tree my son."

I explained that the Egg Tree is a secret thing in the ground under our town and I only told about it because Judge Nagle said I had to make this statement with the whole truth. I was ashamed to tell it, except less so now on account of the Egg Tree has found me again where I sleep in the spare room at Sheriff and Mrs. Sheriff Fader's house. There is a little root coming out of the heater grill in the floor. It says to me, "Do not fear."

The Catholic man is excited about the Egg Tree only he asked me just to call it a Tree only, but I will not be a liar. I have told many lies many times so as not to get a yelling or maybe a whipping from Daddy, but this is a big thing. It is okay to be a liar about who ate the last candy bar or why Daddy's air mattress got a burn hole in it but it is not about important stuff. So I will still say, "Egg Tree."

And I don't think this is something Jesus cares about very much anyway.

That night was cold and wet. See I remembered without reading back so you didn't have to wait. I got to the square where the County Courthouse was built after they moved the County Seat to Ranger Rock from Niffle on account of no railroad in Niffle. I could see that Fentress was there, dancing around like a horse in a rodeo. He was happy to see Lookie Glass that was there with Sparky Surtees and the Must Hill Gang.

If you are not from Ranger Rock, Texas then you don't know Must Hill is in south county near Niffle. Sparky Surtees is a bad man who lives there with lots of motorcycles and dogs and big hairy men with leather jackets. Sometimes they come to Ranger Rock and Sheriff Fader has words with them. The words are mostly bad ones and every once in a while the state troopers come and arrest lots of them.

These big men with motorcycles are the Must Hill Gang and they come with Sparky like fleas come with a dog. And the Mexican wrestlers Jaime Norte and Los Hermanos Gigantescos are there with their masks on.

These are the guys that call Daddy and Fore and me and Fred and Hines the Odd so we call them the Bad. It's like that movie except we're the Odd, the Bad and there ain't no Ugly really so it's not much like that movie I guess. And I am watching them from Center Street that runs into the square which is also State Highway 39. The Bad are bursting in the windows of Virgil's Mercantile, Liquor and Pawn.

"They knocked down the bridge over Rainbow Crick," said Fore who walked up behind me.

"Yow," I said. "You scared me."

Fore had his strong gloves on and his special belt and the hammer that Hines must of gave back to him. I turned my back to the square and looked around and we were all there. Daddy had his raven mask and Hines had his band uniform and Fred just stood there naked in the snow with a big smile like when he won five dollars on the scratch cards down at the Circle K. And I was real proud to be Odd because when all the town was sleeping in their beds and the lights were out and the water was rising we Odd were out there to save the town.

Daddy yelled at me, "Don't yell so loud."

Behind us I heard a big growl that was like a train engine at the siding. I knew it was Fentress and we was in trouble.

#

Wednesday [the] 25th.

After that problem with the reporters today Judge Nagle said, "You can't talk to any one unless Sheriff Fader or myself says it is okay." And I said, "Not even Missus Sheriff Fader?"

And Judge Nagle she sighed real big and she said, "Strangers, Vidor. Don't talk to strangers." And I said, "But Sheriff Fader says there is no one stranger than me and I talk to me all the time."

Then they had another big fight like about the miracle I am supposed to have done on Deputy Feist. Only this time Judge Nagle called Sheriff Fader rude names. Not big rude like go to the principal's office but more rude than I would have been. And Mrs. Sheriff Fader laughed her ass off and said, "You are both being silly." But I promised only I would talk to people I already know and only meet new people if Judge or Sheriff introduced me proper first.

And it was cold that night. The more it gets away from when this was the more that cold is what I remember as the main thing. The egg set to thumping in my pocket like the stamp press down at the Double Iron Machine Shop and I could hear the Egg Tree whispering in my head and it said some weird stuff right then.

"Ezer," said the Egg Tree in my head. "A rise Ezer. Though much reduced a rise Ezer and meet Ranger Rock." It said more crazy stuff like that, and it all sounded like how the speeches before Election Day sound and stuff when I vote for Sheriff Fader and Judge Nagle and the mayor and whoever else Daddy tells me to. My head ached from it and the egg throbbed in my pocket more until I got a bruise I could see later on my leg.

I looked at Fentress and he was like a giant wolf that had gone and swallowed the moon. His eyes glowed yellow and he grew and grew. The Egg Tree whispered to me and told me secrets about myself. And I felt myself be strong and big like Fentress which I've never been on account of being not quite right as they used to say at school.

I took the egg from my pocket, which it tore my jeans to do it on account of it was getting bigger. I took that egg and I touched it to Daddy and Fore and Hines and Fred just like I touched it to Deputy Feist and they all grew and glowed like Fentress did.

Like I felt me doing too.

Daddy grew into his raven mask and one of his eyes squinted shut and he looked so much wiser than he ever did. Fore's arms got real big like he was working out all in one minute and he slapped his hammer in his hand till it rang like thunder when you're sleeping in a box car on a summer afternoon. And Hines got tall and his eyes got squinty like if he looked he could see forever and the bugle in his hand became a great golden horn. And Fred just glowed like the sun till he was lighting up the square. And the egg was warm in my hand and my head opened up and I felt real smart for the only time in my life, and strong as the stones at the heart of the world. That was good.

Hines blew on his great golden horn and lightning split the sky. We was all golden. The Odd walked into the square to meet the Bad in front of Virgil's Mercantile, Liquor and Pawn. I didn't have no weapon but just the egg, but the Egg Tree was in my heart and in my head.

Fentress ran at Daddy and took him in the chest to knock him down. I jumped up onto the dog's back with the egg in my hand. Fentress had Daddy on the ground. His big paws wouldn't both fit on Daddy's chest so Fentress had one out to one side. I grabbed his ear with my teeth and bit and conked him on the head with the egg.

Daddy was screaming, "Get it off me. Ow ow." Fentress didn't like me to bite his ear so he started to twist which was like the ground shaking on account of he was so big. I cracked him on the head again with the egg and it sparkled. Fentress fell like he was poleaxed, right on top of Daddy. I knew I wasn't big enough to move him so I kicked the dog for luck and ran into the square. I prayed Daddy would be okay.

Lookie Glass and Hines Dell were fighting. Hines swang his great golden horn like a sword and I could see Lookie was bleeding. So was Hines from Lookie's bowie knife. Sparky Surtees and the Must Hill Gang had their bikes going to ride circles around Fred Ayer. I could see Jaime Norte and Los Hermanos Gigantescos chasing Fore around a corner but I had to help Fred on account of he was in the most danger.

I ran at Sparky as he came circling around. He caught me in his headlight and turned his motorcycle straight at me. The Egg Tree said more stuff I didn't understand even though it had made me clever. Weird words it was screaming in my head. In my hand its little egg started glowing like Fred was and then I had all the time and strength in the world. I stepped to the left of the bike as Sparky came at me and cocked him right on the head with the little glowing egg.

\#

Monday [the] 30th.

I am in the county jail in the Sheriffs' Station. Mister Hale the County Attorney says I confessed to killing Sparky Surtees and Daddy but I know it wasn't me and even though almost all the Bad and Odd died, I was doing the right thing. After they get done trying me, I am going to state jail somewhere far from here. Judge Nagle is sad for me.

Missus Sheriff Fader says I am a liar now too. Because he is my only friend that is left, Deputy Feist has snuck the tape recorder to me one last time.

Hines and Lookie were both dead from their fight though Sheriff says he can't find the knife Hines used. He says I am a liar about the great golden horn but Deputy Feist whispered to me they found a bugle squashed under Lookie's body. Feist is nice to me now that his wife says

I saved his life. Fred is in the hospital in Kerrville and Sheriff Fader arrested who was left of the Must Hill Gang good and proper that night.

I am sorry about Fore but at least he did save the town. He stole back Judge Nagle's boat where the extra dynamite wound up and blew the levee downstream to drain the town. He blew himself up too.

They can't charge me for everything but they say I was responsible. I tell them it was the Egg Tree but now everyone knows I am a liar and sick and must be sent away. But I did the right thing and helped to save Ranger Rock from the Bad. And it was a good thing on account of the state money for the flood and the newspaper stories and now Deputy Feist says things will be better in Ranger Rock than before.

The six days of snow the radio now is calling the Thimble Winter on account of it was so short. I bet soon no one will remember the Odd but me. I love Daddy and I love Fore and I even love Hines and Fred and I will always miss them.

If she remembers me maybe Nana King will send me picture books at the state jail. I can wait. Someday the Egg Tree will find me there and make me strong and smart again.

NAKED AND HOMELESS
ON GOLGOTHA

Wing-Back Woman hissed from beneath Oatis' dresser. "Oatis-boy, you, listen up."

Heat-stunned flies clung to the cream-colored ceiling. Oatis lay on the narrow iron-railed bed, shuffling cards on his chest. He didn't play—Pastor Simpkins said it was sinful, and besides Oatis didn't know how—but he loved the crisp feel of the deck between his fingers.

"I hear you, Wing-Back Woman, ma'am," he whispered. Oatis had to be quiet because the ward nurse got mad when he talked to the People. He was respectful because Wing-Back Woman had a sharp tongue and a hard view of him. At least she talked straight, and Oatis thought she liked him.

Wing-Back Woman scuttled out from under the dresser and crawled up the leg of Oatis' bed, glossy brown carapace contrasting with the chipped beige metal. Antennae twitching, she stood on the white muslin sheet, where it folded down the required eight inches over his blanket. "Oatis-boy, I tell you this truth. There's a miracle gonna happen on top of Scully Hill. You best get your skinny ass out of bed and beat feet on over there."

Oatis stopped shuffling. He always tried to be polite, but he didn't like being told what to do. He looked Wing-Back Woman in her faceted eyes and said, "I don't reckon a long walk in this here heat will do me much good, Wing-Back Woman."

"Oatis-boy, I ain't tellin' you no more. Only once you gonna get this chance. Just go see what there is to see. Witnessing a miracle's like taking a journey—it will change your life." She rustled her wings at him. "But if you just want to set here like a broody hen for the rest of your born days, that's your business." Wing-Back Woman skittered down off the bed without waiting for an answer.

"A miracle," said Oatis to himself. "Like a journey." Pastor Simpkins talked about miracles a lot, but they always seemed silly, bushes on fire or fishes doing arithmetic in baskets someplace far away. And he didn't want to take a journey or change his life. Oatis liked being in the State Hospital—it was safe and clean here. But a miracle might be interesting. He might learn something. If not, he could always come home again.

Oatis sat up, stretched, then placed the cards in his top dresser drawer. He laced his blue canvas shoes and set out to find Dr. Canady for a day pass. "Thank you, ma'am," Oatis said to the empty room as he closed the door. Best not to vex any of the People. They were his only friends.

#

"No, Oatis," Dr. Canady said in his Yankee voice, "no pass. Besides, you shouldn't be out in that August heat. You'll dehydrate or worse. The rec center's air-conditioned. Go play ping-pong or something." The doctor flipped a paper in the folder he was holding.

Nobody ever listened to what Oatis wanted. Oatis started to rock his body back and forth, fighting the moan that rose deep inside him. Tears stinging his eyes and a hot rush in his cheeks, Oatis bent his head to speak. The words bounced off his chest. "Judge Horner said I could go out days."

"Oatis." Dr. Canady sighed. "Judge Horner doesn't know you like I know you. You don't do well on your own dealing with people on the outside. Look, I can put you on the mall bus Friday." The doctor forced his voice into a jolly rhythm. "McDonald's? You can eat French fries and watch the pretty girls ice skate."

"You got to let me go out," muttered Oatis. His fingernails dug into his palms, so he hid his hands behind his back where Dr. Canady couldn't see them. "I'm just gonna go for a walk. Won't see nobody. Won't talk to nobody."

"I've got no official reason to deny you, Oatis. You haven't had any demerits in months." Dr. Canady made a clicking noise, like he was thinking. "All right. I'll make out a day pass. Don't be long, and turn back as soon as things don't feel right for you. And Oatis, it's hot as hell out there. Promise me you'll at least get some bottled water from the cafeteria?"

#

Oatis carried a case of bottles two miles to Scully Hill in the Texas summer heat, the heavy cardboard box banging into his thighs with every step. Once he crossed the barbed wire and headed up the hill, the walking got tougher. Clustered burrs from the beggar's lice smeared his jeans, while thorned stretch vine yanked at his ankles.

"Where you going with that water?"

Oatis stopped and set down the box. He was halfway up the hill, and the water was heavy, so taking a rest was good. Dr. Canady would approve. Oatis looked around to see White-Stripe Man preening on a small branch in a dead pecan tree.

"Howdy, sir," Oatis said. His mama had taught him to show respect. "I'm on my way up Scully Hill to see what there is to see."

"What for? Nothing up there." White-Stripe Man burrowed for mites in the feathers under one wing.

White-Stripe Man was rude. The People never lied to Oatis—that was why he liked them—but they could be mighty snappish. "Nothing up there yet, maybe," he said, "but Wing-Back Woman says there's a miracle coming."

White-Stripe Man flipped his head back up and laughed. "You listen to Wing-Back Woman? Hah! She's an old fraud. Me, I'm out here in the fields. I know the score."

Oatis drew one arm across his face to wipe off the sweat. He was powerful thirsty, and White-Stripe Man's argument made his head hurt. "What score?"

White-Stripe Man glared at Oatis. "I tell you there ain't nothing on Scully Hill except dirt, grass and sky."

Oatis knew he was being mocked, so he picked up his case of water without even taking the time to drink some. "Good day to you, White-Stripe Man," he said, then walked onward.

Why would one of the People lie to him?

#

From the county road, Scully Hill had looked to be just a big rock knob, not too high. Up here on the hill, Oatis could swear he'd been climbing for an hour. Loose gray rocks slipped under his feet, occasionally giving way to stone shelves with grassy clumps growing in tiny, eroded pits. White-Stripe Man flew back and forth above him, jeering.

Oatis finally came to the top of the hill. This was where Wing-Back Woman had sent him to see what could be seen. What he saw was three cedar crosses, papery red bark over yellow wood, charred and toppled to the ground, with a circle of grass trampled around them. A naked man curled near the middle one, half-hidden in the grass.

Oatis set his case of water bottles down and approached the stranger. Oatis summoned his courage and asked, "You okay, mister?"

The man was short, with brown skin and long, curly black hair. He hadn't bathed in a while, and he looked to be sick. The stranger's forehead was bloody, as were his hands. "I am well enough," he said with a tight smile, "although I thirst."

Oatis opened his case of water. He offered a bottle to the stranger.

The stranger took it and fumbled with the plastic bottle for a moment without opening it. "What is this?"

"Here, I'll help." Oatis took the bottle back, popped the cap, and returned it.

The stranger drank. "Thank you," he said after a few moments.

"You're welcome," Oatis said. Wing-Back Woman's promises and White-Stripe Man's lies swirled in his head, blending together into an irritating mush, the way most conversations did. He was angry at the People for confusing him. "Are you my miracle?"

"I am every man's miracle," said the stranger, his smile more genuine this time.

Oatis had never seen one of the People who looked like a regular person, but he wondered if this Miracle-Man was just that—a new kind of People. "But you're here for me? To be my miracle?"

"I am both messenger and message."

The stranger didn't look like a message. Oatis knew messages came on pieces of paper, like letters in the mail or a note from the Admin Office. That was the kind of thing Wing-Back Woman would say, when she was feeling chatty. . . . "Even though you don't look like it, you are one of the People," Oatis announced.

The stranger sat up, leaning against the toppled cedar cross. "Who else is of the People?"

"White-Stripe Man," Oatis said, pointing to his companion in the sky. "Wing-Back Woman, who lives under my dresser at the State Hospital. Green Boy, who lives in the pond along our back fence. You know. *People.*"

"What about the woman who prepares your food, or the physician who treats your illness?"

"Well . . . " Oatis stared down at his own chest. The People didn't like these kinds of questions, so neither did Oatis. The stranger was going to make him angry soon. "They're regular persons, like me. The People are different. Dr. Canady says you all aren't real, but, well, here we are."

White-Stripe Man landed on the cross furthest from the stranger. He looked at Oatis. "Damned straight we're different. And I told you there was nothing up here but grass and sky."

"He is here." Oatis nodded at the stranger.

White-Stripe Man shrugged his wings. "He's crazy. He doesn't count."

"I'm crazy, too," Oatis pointed out. "Dr. Canady says I wouldn't be able to talk to you otherwise."

"Nor him," said White-Stripe Man with a stab of his beak at the stranger. White-Stripe Man fluffed his feathers and settled more comfortably on the burnt cedarwood.

"I'm not crazy," said the stranger. "I belong to God."

"Pastor Simpkins says we're all God's children." Oatis offered the stranger another water bottle. "Nothing crazy about that, I reckon."

"I'm dying on a distant hill even now," said the stranger.

"You're sitting with me on top of Scully Hill," said Oatis. "You look messed up, not dead."

"You're both crazy," said White-Stripe Man. "Sonny here is looking for a way out of the world. Oatis is looking for a way in. You should switch."

Oatis thought about his comfortable bed with his favorite feather pillow, and the Coke machine down the hall, and Tuesday Double Jello Nights at the cafeteria. "Why did you say that?" he whispered to his chest. "I like my life. I don't want to give it up, not even to go back into the world."

"I'm not here to trade with you," said Sonny. "I was sent to redeem you. I have been sent to redeem every man everywhere, but only a few are privileged to see me outside their hearts."

"Redeem?" Oatis asked. "Like an empty Coke can?"

White-Stripe Man laughed so hard he nearly fell off the cedar cross. Oatis glared as heat rushed to his cheeks.

Sonny shook a finger at White-Stripe Man, who turned into an ordinary mockingbird, squawked, and flew away.

"What did you do that for?" Tears burned in Oatis' eyes as he looked back up at Sonny. "White-Stripe Man was my friend."

"He was not helping you."

"It don't matter. It weren't for you to change him like that." Oatis looked up into the sky, but the bird was gone.

Sonny sighed just like Dr. Canady did when he'd been talking to Oatis for too long. "I didn't change *him*, Oatis. I changed you. *He* was always a mockingbird."

Oatis crossed his arms. He felt hard, certain, in a way he'd never felt before, the tears receding as quickly as they had come. The world was different, his anger shifting into focus with hard, red frames. "Change me back."

"You're better off."

"What do you know?" Oatis was shouting, for the first time in years. "You're naked and homeless on top of a hill. Who the heck gave you power to steal my world? I hate this damned *miracle*!"

Sonny looked sad, almost desperate. "Don't you see, I've given you back the world, redeemed you from the voices inside your head."

Oatis kicked over the open case of bottled water. "Go to hell, Miracle-Man. I've had enough of you." He jumped on the toppled case, cracking the plastic bottles within and releasing a pool of water to soak into the parched soil.

"Are you just going to leave me here?" Sonny looked smaller.

Without answering, Oatis turned and walked back down the hill with long, angry strides. The afternoon heat seared into his head, his neck, his shoulders.

"Wait," cried Sonny from behind him.

Oatis stopped, stared back with narrow eyes. His face felt pinched by anger. "What?"

"I'm sorry," said Sonny. He had one of the cracked bottles in his hand. "I did not see your madness as a state of grace. Let me help." Sonny dipped two fingers in the water pouring from his palm, pink with blood, and reached out toward Oatis as if to touch him from a distance.

A mockingbird circled down to land near Oatis, cocking its head from side to side to examine him with each eye. Oatis looked at the dusty rocks between his feet, where a little wolf spider scuttled through the dirt. What kind of retard was he, talking to the animals? He glared back up at Sonny. "I just wanted to see you and go home again. You took away what I had, but you can't give it back. It's not the same." He started to cry again, harsh, angry tears that burned his cheeks. "Now I know how stupid I was."

Oatis crushed the wolf spider under his canvas shoe, grabbed a rock and threw it toward Sonny, who yelped as it struck his forehead. Oatis walked into the August haze, another sharp rock ready in hand. Anywhere but the State Hospital, he thought. Anywhere at all.

There were no People anymore, just humming cicadas and dispirited cowbirds.

ANCIENT WINE

There's an art to finding these little caves in the Texas Hill Country. Even with Reddy Max's directions, this one took hours. And the day was so hot even the bugs had given up. Finally I squeezed my middle-aged gut into a limestone gap, using a stick to probe for rattlers. Inside, reflected sunlight lent a dusty glow to the blessedly cool air.

That was when I saw the old man.

He snored, naked but for a ragged blanket and a long beard, with an empty bottle of Mad Dog 20/20 next to him. How'd he survive in here? I'd hiked across a mile of mesquite, cactus and fractured rock. There wasn't a drop of open water out there, and precious little to eat.

I'm no burglar, so I turned away, pausing to give him a last glance. The old man stared back, eyes catching the light like a dog outside the campfire circle. Or maybe a wolf—something in his gaze took my breath. "*Kyrie*," he said. Greek.

I refused to fear his nakedness, his filth, his wild eyes. "You okay?"

He hawked, spat, stood. He was short, wide, and well hung—and long past his last bath. "Eh . . . fine. What day?" Unlike his first word, the accent was not quite Greek.

"Uh, Saturday," I said, forcing myself between the rocks. I was stuck. I exhaled and sucked in my gut.

He scratched his pubes. "Twelve or nineteen?"

Twelve or nineteen? I made few more inches, then stopped hard. I'd never been truly stuck before, and it scared the hell out of me. My voice shook. "It's the twenty-sixth." Was that what he meant?

He looked at the empty bottle with an ancient sorrow, then tossed it behind him. I didn't hear it smash. He grinned, teeth like daggers. "Buy an old man a drink?"

"Sure," I whimpered, trapped between the rocks and his gaze. Tender as a mother's hands, the limestone released me.

#

My ribs ached, my shirt was torn, panic echoed in my pulse. Blanket around his waist, the old man walked with me. His bare feet looked tougher than my jump boots.

Scrambling over a ridge, I was startled to notice the old man now wore blue jeans, the blanket over his shoulders like a serape. He'd been beside me stride-for-stride since leaving the cave. Where the hell had he gotten the jeans?

He smiled. His teeth looked less pointed in daylight, and his beard seemed more tame. "Right," I whispered.

"Wine," he said.

#

We rattled up to the Circle K in my Eldorado ragtop, squealing to a halt in a stench of unburnt fuel. The old man stepped out over his door. That was when I realized the blanket was actually a pelt. Goat?

The teen counter zombie didn't blink at no shirt, no shoes. The old man marched straight to the cooler, grabbed half a dozen bottles of Mad Dog, and headed out. I stepped to the register as the kid finally woke up to shout, "Hey!"

I followed an unaccountable impulse to lay down two twenties. "Forget it."

He shrugged, the twenties disappeared, and his eyes reglazed. I left, wondering what had possessed me to start throwing my meager cash around on an old bum.

#

Behind the store, we leaned against the urine-stained cinderblock wall. The Texas Alcoholic Beverage Commission sign above our heads informed us that consuming liquor on premises was a felony. Selling this stuff should be a felony—it tasted like piss Kool-Aid and grain alcohol, overlaid with a frightening sweetness. I took another deep swig.

"No one knows how to make wine anymore," the old man said. He'd lost his accent, voice now Hollywood-hearty.

"And you do?" Alcoholic belligerence rose within me. This stuff was hitting me fast.

"It's all sweet, light essence of grape now. *Fruity.* I really should do something about California." He grinned, teeth suddenly perfect like a Yuppie dentist's advertising model, and stuck out his hand. "Call me Deimos."

"Deimos. Sure." My Classics Ph.D. was finally paying off. Deimos was Panic, one of the dogs of War. But with all the wine, he was more Dionysus than Deimos. I shook his hand. "Fine, you're Panic, I'll be Fear. Phobos, charmed I'm sure. Where the hell is Ares, anyway?"

"Don't ask." He hitched himself a little higher against the wall. "You weren't looking for me, were you?"

"Reddy Max sent me," I said precisely. My friend the wino, lived in a dumpster behind my apartment. "I was looking for arrowheads. Was finding you a bad thing?"

"Depends." He tossed his empty. No shattering noise from the tall grass near our feet. It was like his bottle vanished in flight. "Know any women? Winos are easiest."

Suddenly I didn't feel nearly as drunk. What was I doing with this guy, and why didn't I just walk away?

But I didn't. That made me wonder if I could.

#

We drove east on US 290, through Oak Hill, on into Austin. Deimos wore my tux shirt, from the bowling bag I keep in the trunk for special occasions. I was sweating like a Death Row inmate. Around me, the Eldorado gradually regained its lost youth. Torn upholstery was made whole. The big crack in the windshield shrank before my eyes. The right-pulling wobble in the steering vanished. I was afraid to look at my gut. My waistband felt loose.

It would have cost me thousands to have someone do what Deimos seemed to be doing to my car all by himself.

"Um, Deimos . . . " Or was it really Dionysus? The old wine god had a strange reputation, responsible for everything from tragedy to the Maenads—death by fingernail, as it were, women rending men and beasts limb from limb.

"Yeah?" He stared at the passing cityscape of quick oil change franchises and fast food restaurants with the enthusiastic indifference of a Labrador retriever.

"What . . . ah . . . what's happening?"

His eyes had that glow again as he glanced at me. "We're cruising for chicks, remember?"

"Uh huh." I patted the steering wheel with my fingertips. One of us was nuts. I didn't like either option.

"In style," Deimos added. "Cruising in style."

#

We idled the car through downtown alleys until a woman sleeping behind a dumpster struck Deimos' fancy. He jumped out and whispered in her ear for a while until she woke up and argued. "No funny stuff!" she screeched. "One's enough for me. At least, one at a time." Her laugh was worse than her screeching.

Our new friend looked sixty, which on the street probably meant thirty-five or forty. If she had teeth left, I couldn't see them. She had more clothes on her than the sale rack at Wal-Mart.

Deimos helped her into the back seat, then got in front. "Back to my place, Phobos," he said. "And give her fifty dollars."

"Yeah, in a minute." He was serious about this woman thing, apparently. I needed to think. We seemed to be crossing a line here, from a crazy-magical drinking binge to something truly frightening.

I swung the Caddy out onto Sixth Street. The car was now midnight blue, with a subtle black flame job on the front and enough chrome *chingaderos* to shame a crack dealer. The side pipes rumbled like a Harley. The fuzzy dice matched the paint job, black pips on midnight blue. My radio worked for the first time since I'd owned the beast, but it would only play some wailing Middle Eastern stuff.

With a sigh, I reached into my pocket and came out with a roll that could choke a pig. I was so surprised I dropped the cash onto the floor. Deimos picked it up, peeled off a fifty, and gave it to the lady wino.

He'd almost bought me off with the car, but the money was too weird. I slammed on the brakes. The car slewed to a halt in the center lane as horns blared. "No!" I shouted. "You are not going to do *whatever* to that woman. Turn her into a Maenad or make a rite of spring or some crap."

"What are you complaining about?" He seemed amused, not angry. His date leaned forward to slap the top of the front seat, cackling gleefully.

"This . . . it's wrong. You don't belong here, in Texas, in the twenty-first century. You're fucking Dionysus, you're supposed to be wandering the olive groves and vineyards of Asia Minor." I flipped the fuzzy dice, waved at the car. "Our world doesn't work this way. Put her back the way she was, put me and the car back the way we were, and go back to your damned cave."

"Walter," said Reddy Max. My personal wino, who normally lived in the alley behind my house, had appeared out of nowhere to stand next to the driver door with one hand on my elbow. His palsy was in sudden remission. "Relax. This is good."

The car was surrounded by winos. The old woman breathed close behind me, whispering, "Oh, lucky man." She tongued my ear.

I punched down the accelerator, knocking ragged men aside to run the red light half a block distant at Lavaca. A crowd of screaming winos gave chase in my review mirror, but that Cadillac 500-inch V-8 drew us forward like time's arrow.

I crossed the intersection at Rio Grande doing about sixty, narrowly missing a Cap Metro bus. In the mirror, I could see the winos keeping up—Hades' own Olympic track team.

"Get out of the car! He'll kill you!" I screamed at the woman licking my neck. Her hands slipped inside my shirt. Distracted by visions of flesh-rending Maenads, I glanced over at Dionysus.

He was laughing, waving another bottle of Mad Dog. A quick look over my shoulder showed the winos gaining on us.

How to beat him? I was out of options, going seventy-five miles an hour through downtown Austin. Dionysus, god of wine—he died every year, torn apart by Hera, or in some stories the Titans, to be reborn in the spring like the fruit of the vine. I didn't have any Titans handy, but the god seemed to be investing a lot of power in those wine bottles he kept tossing into the ether. I could do something about that.

"Time for a miracle, big boy," I said as I let go of the wheel at about eighty miles an hour coming up on the Lamar light. It was red, and there were no open lanes, but I didn't care. I just wanted to distract him long enough to stop him. I lunged for Dionysus' bottle of Mad Dog, snatching it from his hands as the car bucked.

He looked surprised, but his eyes filled with that glowing fire I'd seen before. We lifted smoothly into the air, soaring over the line of traffic as sirens screamed in the distance. I swung the wine bottle like I was going to hit him, then released it to spin across the door into the open air below us.

Dionysus' voice boomed Classical Greek imprecations like thunder in the summer sky. My eardrums felt fit to rupture. I was surprised the car hadn't yet wrecked when I heard the wine bottle shatter like the breaking of the world.

The Eldorado landed on top of the Waterloo Records building without rolling over. The car spun like a duck on ice before slamming into a huge HVAC unit in the middle of the flat roof. Radiator fluid spewed as sparks arced off the HVAC. The lady wino and I tumbled out of the car just as the engine caught fire.

All the winos, including Dionysus's date, did a big fade before the cops pulled up. My car was a total loss by the time they got it down off the roof. What the fire and the collision hadn't gotten, Dionysus had reclaimed—faded paint, torn upholstery were restored. Even my big gut had come back. Somehow I wound up holding the goatskin.

They cited me for half a dozen traffic violations, but as none of the witnesses could agree on exactly how the car had gotten on the roof, the cops eventually let me go.

#

It all made a weird kind of sense. The gods had moved west, just like the seats of power, throughout history. Greek gods were born in Asia Minor, came to the Peloponnese, then on to Rome. Why not Texas? It looks a lot like their old Levantine home, after all. And libations are the oldest sacrament—wine in particular being Dionysus' domain. Especially the acrid, bitter wine of ancient olive groves, dark seas and the thousand-ship fleet. And every street drunk in the world was his acolyte.

Sometimes I throw the god's old goatskin over my shoulder and go stare at convenience store wine until the cops make me leave. Sometimes I wander downtown looking for women in the alleys, lost in dreams of dancing with them across sun-blasted hills. I fear I am the springtime coming of the god.

Winos follow me everywhere I go.

SPARROWS,
TWO FOR A PENNY

"It's almost Christmas." Eleanor sighed, wishing for the miracle that never came. "We should get Johnnie something."

Henry sat on the ragged tweed sleeper couch, beer in one hand, TV remote in the other, watching a fishing show. "He's not going to make it much past New Year's. Why waste the money?"

Johnnie's cancer had eaten their lives. They'd sold the doublewide to pay medical bills. Then Henry had begged the use of his late grandpa Wessex's rusting mobile home, which his cousin Norman moved onto Henry and Eleanor's over-mortgaged land. It was a cheaply-paneled tin box that reeked of old industrial adhesives and cat urine. Even in December, it could be hotter than hell in the little living room. The pervasive odors of Johnnie's slow passing were all that belonged to them anymore.

"He's still our boy." Eleanor sighed, too tired to argue. Their fights were long over, ended in mutual defeat. Richard hadn't come back from Desert Storm. Geoffrey ran off to the streets with the Latin Kings. Eleanor figured they wouldn't see him again this side of a prison wall. Escaped into distant marriages, the girls never wrote. She had only Johnnie, guts rotting from the inside out—the doctors called it "metastasized Stage IV colon cancer."

And she had Henry, lost in his beer and his satellite TV. Sometimes he still remembered they were married. Life had stolen away her beauty and his wit, leaving them to broil slowly in a trailer reeking of rotting child. She missed the man he she married, pitied the man he had become.

"Yeah, he was our boy," Henry finally said over a commercial. He looked away from the television for a moment to stare at Eleanor. She could swear there was nothing in Henry's eyes but flickering blue glare. "Our boy could have been anything. Now he's just dying."

#

Twelve years old, thought Eleanor as she chopped onions in the kitchenette. Who the hell got colon cancer when they were twelve? Her bitter anger had been enough to turn her away from God, from her church. Thirteen now, Johnnie would never see fourteen. The last of her children slipped away on their family's ruinous tide. Henry's TV blared mattress advertisements as her eyes watered.

Enough, she thought, no more of this. There was nothing else she could do for Johnnie except to set him free. Henry was . . . Henry. Eleanor wiped the blade clean and stepped around the edge of the counter with the knife dangling loose in her hand.

#

Afterward she changed out of her ruined clothes and drove Henry's Buick Regal over to the Fontevrault Bible Church. The parking lot was empty except for Sister Blanche's blue Aries with the red fender under the billboard of the sinners quailing before the power of God. "PRAY FOR YOUR LIFE," the sign read in letters taller than Eleanor.

Fontevrault had doors like a high school—brown metal with a skinny window above the handle, wire-woven security glass offering a filtered view of the promised freedom on the other side. Eleanor pushed her way into the little metal building.

"Sister Eleanor," said Sister Blanche. White-haired, severe, wearing a plain blue cotton dress, she sat on a folding chair repairing a box fan with a collection of tools scattered around her. The white-paneled room was crowded with folding chairs and plastic flowers. A large, plain cross hung over a banquet table with an enormous Bible and two more pots of plastic flowers. "It's been a while since we've seen you in the Lord's house. Welcome."

"Sister Blanche." Eleanor nodded. She stared at the cross, daring God to take a good, hard look at her life.

For a time, the silence was interrupted only by the clicking of Blanche's screwdriver. Eventually, the older woman set her tools down. "What can I do for you today?"

"I want to talk to God."

Blanche studied Eleanor, shaking her head slowly. "Then pray, child. He hears every sparrow fall."

"I've read Matthew, Sister," snapped Eleanor. "Sparrows are two for a penny. And I've seen how much good prayer did for me. I want the real thing. I want God's personal attention."

"You know it doesn't work that way."

Eleanor paced around the church. "My life was supposed to be different. I was born in France. I was beautiful, all my aunts said I'd marry a prince—Henry." She laughed, a sound more like choking. "Henry. Now I'm fifty-five, living in a junked trailer in Caldwell County, Texas, my kids are gone, or dead . . . " She kicked at a folding chair. "I want Johnnie back. God took his colon. Johnnie wasn't done with it yet."

Sister Blanche laid a cool hand on Eleanor's cheek. "God hears every prayer, child. But we must find His answers within ourselves." She gently kissed the side of Eleanor's face. "Go home to Henry. Love Johnnie while you still have him."

Eleanor began to cry. It was too late for love.

#

In the days that followed, the trailer was so quiet that she finally turned the television back on. It would keep her mind off the stench of bodies, which even onions couldn't mask. The channels seemed to be different since she had smashed Henry's remote.

Eleanor saw that God had taken note of her love, used the television to give her back her family. She kept spotting Henry in the movies, always a king or a general or a dashing cavalry officer. He was young, and witty, and happy in ways she had forgotten he could be. Eleanor loved that Henry on the screen all over again. Richard showed up in a few scenes too, smiling shyly, always lost in the desert with Peter O'Toole or Ernest Borgnine.

Eleanor thanked God in her prayers and kept waiting for Him to complete His gift, to show her Johnnie walking around and smiling, his young body healthy and whole. But her youngest son was camera-shy. She stopped eating, stopped sleeping even, staying in front of the television all the time waiting for Johnnie to come back to her, fearful of missing the miracle of his return.

Her miracle never came, although God eventually did. He found Eleanor in front of the television on the blood-stained couch, a penny clutched in her hand.

ALIENS

MAMA SHE TRUCK

So you're the new guy that bought the Aaronson place out on 61. Welcome to Caldwell County, Texas. Betty sent you over here from the Post Office, huh? Well, I reckon I need to tell you about the bacon-headed kid. Grab a beer, flip over that "Closed" sign on the screen door, and take a seat. No, not that chair, it belongs to the cat.

Never you mind what cat. Chair's as big as it needs to be.

#

Louise Marks comes into my general store two or three times a month. She always has a gaggle of kids with her, runs a foster home for Caldwell County, so the courts keep dumping youngsters on her. I never could see what she gets out of it, except sheer love. She'll come in surrounded by four, five, as many as six or seven kids, every size and color, make copies over here behind the counter.

What? Medical reports, time sheets, I don't know. Court stuff, whatever. Then she'll buy those kids a couple of bags of M&M's, make them count it out fair and square, and off they go.

Louise is an okay looking gal, for all she lives like a nun in an orphanage. Sort of resembles someone's grandmother at about age

forty-five—mouse brown hair in one of them permanents that adds
ten years on her, and a little pair of cat-eye glasses with the rhinestones
on the corner. She always wears jeans and flannel shirts and drives a
big green Chevy step van, like the electricity co-op uses. One of them
kids had painted "Mama She Truck" on the side in drippy white paint.
Louise left it on there. I reckon she likes it. Never did figure exactly
what that means.

So one day she comes in with seven kids that commenced to boiling
up and down the aisles chasing my cat Sammy—who will abide
anything that happens in the store with good cheer except being
picked up and held—and I didn't think nothing of it. Louise runs a
tight ship; none of those kids ever stole nothing, which is more than I
could say for Pastor Martin's brood. Little glue-fingers, the whole
Bible-pounding bunch of them. I stepped aside to let her around the
counter to the copier, and whomp, this kid slams into me, right in the
jewels.

Oh, crap, I about doubled over, breathing hard and holding in some
ripping cuss words. Louise grabbed my shoulder. "You okay, Bert,"
she asked. I could tell she was trying not to laugh.

Head down near my knees, I gasped out that I was fine. Then I
looked up into the yellow eyes of this little bacon-headed kid.

No, not like that. What are you thinking, marbled slabs of fat like
some Dick Tracy villain? No, this kid was green the color of split pea
soup, with two little knobs coming out of his forehead like them hairy
horns on a giraffe. Each knob had reddish-purple crinkly stuff on the
end, about the color of cooked bacon. That's all I could think of,
bacon. Sounds better than calling him the pea-headed kid, doesn't it?
And his eyes, instead of pupils, they had little slits like Sammy's. For
about two seconds I was scared spitless, until I realized how cute he
was.

"Bert," said Louise, "This here's my new boy, Johnnie Smith. You
be real nice to him. He doesn't talk, which is powerful wrong for a kid
as big as he is, so we're helping him out while Judge Sorensen finds his
parents."

I'd about got my breath back at that point, so I straightened partway up and squeezed out kind of a constipated little smile. "Hello there, Bacon-Head," I said. There was something charming about the little guy.

Well, two of the other kids were racing by the counter about then, and the next thing I knew they're all shouting out, "Bacon-Head, Bacon-Head, call Johnnie that, his forehead's red."

"Bert, I will thank you to keep your big mouth shut next time," Louise snapped. But she knew better than to argue with the kids right then and there. The thing had to run its course. Instead, she took little Johnnie Bacon-Head in tow and stepped over to my copier. Sammy followed them over and began rubbing against the bacon-headed kid's legs, which he don't normally do. I guess he liked the kid, too.

I finally handed out free M&Ms to the other six kids to shut them up. I kept a bag aside for the bacon-headed kid too, the kind with peanuts to make up for what I'd said. On the way out the door, Louise glared at me again. "Too much chocolate's bad for them."

Sammy and I watched that old step van rattle off down the Lockhart Highway and figured that was the last I'd seen of the bacon-headed kid. I didn't have the nerve to charge Louise for the copies, neither.

#

The next day, Deputy Hardegree came in to the shop. He's a big, pale man who could break a sweat in a meat locker. Sammy scampered behind the antifreeze soon as the deputy appeared. "Well, howdy, Bert," Hardegree said.

"Deputy." I behave myself, but visits from the law still weren't high on my wish list. "What can I do for you?"

Hardegree isn't a bad sort, but he returned from Desert Storm a few beans shy of a burrito, if you know what I mean. Despite the nervous tic, Sheriff Coleman gave Hardegree his job back, and the dispatchers try to keep him away from the ugly calls. Which means most days he serves papers and writes traffic tickets to people with out-of-state plates.

"Louise Marks been in here?"

"Not since yesterday," I said, wondering what on Earth Hardegree would want with Louise.

He looked at a Polaroid in his hand. "Seems Judge Sorensen gave her temporary custody of some weird kid the INS picked up. Turns out the FBI wants to talk to the little freak real bad. Big mistake losing track of the kid, now there's three or four kinds of Federal agents swarming around the County Courthouse over in Lockhart."

Little freak, my hind foot. I knew Hardegree didn't mean nothing by it, but I still got a bit hot. There wasn't no way that bacon-headed kid was a criminal. "What they want this kid for?"

Hardegree grinned. "Illegal alien."

Yeah, I'll bet. I wasn't giving him nothing now. "Can't help you there, Roddie. She was in, she was out."

"She do anything unusual while she was here?"

Suddenly I didn't want him looking around my copier. Sometimes people make mistakes and throw sheets in the trash. Whatever Louise might have done, I wasn't turning little Johnnie Bacon-Head in. "Got some M&Ms for the kids, that's about it."

Hardegree touched the brim of his hat. "Thank you kindly, Bert." I watched him until his cruiser passed the cottonwood grove at the bend in the road, then scooted over to the copier. Sammy was there ahead of me, batting a wad of paper around next to the trashcan he'd tumped over. I took the paper away from the cat and spread it out on the counter.

Well it was in Chinese or something, all squiggly strokes and stuff, with Louise's little crabby handwriting written in the boxes, thrown out because she'd copied it sideways and cut off about a third of the page. "Smith, Johnnie." "Male." "Approx. 8 years old." "No vacc'n record." I couldn't see where she'd been able to tell which box on the form was for what any more than I could. Louise was a practical woman—I figured she'd made her best guess and forged ahead.

Sammy jumped up on the counter and laid a paw on the crumpled photocopy. I looked at the cat. He stared right back at me, those little slit pupils just like the eyes of the bacon-headed kid. I had to tell Louise the heat was on, warn her, whatever good that might do. When I reached for the phone, Sammy put that paw on my hand, claws just barely pricking my skin.

"Think I should go in person?" I asked the cat.

Sammy hopped off the counter and sauntered toward the door. This from a cat that didn't even like to go outside. He must have really taken to that kid.

I let the cat out, flipped the "Closed" sign, locked up and climbed into my 1978 AMC Pacer wagon—it's a woodie. Me and Sammy headed for Louise's place.

#

She has a big old farmhouse off County Road 294. The green step van was parked outside, along with a rusted blue Ford tractor. The house itself was a two-story frame building leaning about five degrees out of true, held up mostly by the chimney at the west end. Mesquite trees crowded around the building like cattle mobbing a coyote. No kids in sight, no Louise. I parked the Pacer next to the step van and got out. Sammy set to exploring the front yard. Everything was real quiet, so I knocked on the door.

One of her kids answered, which was a relief. I was afraid something might already have happened. This was a little Asian girl I'd seen the last few times Louise had come by the store. The kid looked like her dog had just died.

"Mama Louise around?" I asked.

She nodded, clinging to the doorknob.

Okay, try again. "Can I speak to her?"

She nodded again, still clinging.

Time to be more specific. "Can I come inside and speak to her now?"

The Asian girl nodded, then stepped back, away from the door.

Sammy slipped in around my ankles. I'd never been inside Louise's place, so I didn't know what to expect. Whatever vague notions I'd had about foster mothers and halfway houses full of vinyl furniture vanished in an explosion of chintz, satin and crystal. The floor creaked beneath my feet, but it was covered with a nice Persian rug. Oval-framed photos of prune-faced nineteenth century farmwives hung surrounded by kids' watercolors, all of them at a five-degree angle to the striped wallpaper. A sideboy held a display of gold-rimmed china over which my mother, God rest her soul, would have had the vapors.

How Louise kept all those kids in this house furnished out like a museum was a mystery only the good Lord could plumb. I was afraid of breaking something just standing still in the middle of the room.

Ahead of me, the Asian girl slipped through the dining room and past a swinging door that had to lead to the kitchen. I followed her.

The kitchen about matched the front room for lace, wall art and valuable-looking old woman stuff. Louise sat in front of an enamel-topped table staring at a black rotary-dial telephone like it would bite her. She seemed fit to cry. All seven kids clustered around her, the little bacon-headed kid right in the middle of the group. They looked like they'd just been invited to a funeral. Sammy scampered over and began winding between the ankles of the bacon-headed kid's high-water jeans.

"Louise?"

She looked up me. Her whole face quivered, straining to fly apart in tears. "I think I'm in trouble, Bert."

Well, that was what I had come out here to tell her —and to see the bacon-headed kid again, of course—but it wasn't what she needed to hear. "It'll be okay," I lied, though we both knew better. "You haven't done nothing wrong."

Louise shook her head. "There's Federal agents coming right now. If I don't cooperate, they'll bring me up on immigration charges." She glanced at Ramon, one of the kids who'd been with her a while.

"I know what they want," I said. "Roddie Hardegree came by the store asking about Johnnie Smith."

Her blue eyes flashed, dangerous and pretty. "What did you tell him, Bertram Spinning?"

I put my hands up. "Whoa, Louise. Nothing, nothing. I came out here to see you as soon as Roddie left."

Louise shuddered, but she held it in. "Judge Sorensen's going to take these kids away from me, and he isn't going to give me any more. Bert, I didn't do anything."

I pulled the crumpled paper out my pocket, the one from the trashcan. "You filling out forms for the Chinese?"

She snatched it out of my hand. "You've got no call to go snooping in other's people's trash, Bert!"

"It was *my* trash. That ain't snooping."

Louise glared at me, gritting her teeth. "You know what I mean. Johnnie's foreign—" She broke off, glanced at the bacon-headed kid, who smiled shyly. He had Sammy in his arms now, of all things. "Just look for yourself, Bert," she hissed. "This here's paperwork from his home country. His parents had a little accident, left him on his own. We couldn't just put him on the next airplane out."

Outside, a helicopter buzzed the house, the ratcheting blades making the old windows shake. All of us glanced at the ceiling, me, Louise and the kids, as if there were wisdom written in that pressed tin.

This was not right, so not right that I couldn't even stand it. I'd come over to warn Louise, but that wasn't enough any more. She and the kid needed help. "Come on, Johnnie," I said, holding out my hand.

The bacon-headed kid smiled, shook his head, clutching Sammy. For once in its life that animal was happy to be held by someone. Crud, I thought. What a time for loving kindness to break out.

Louise touched my arm. "What are you going to do, Bert?"

"Give me his paperwork," I said. "Me and him and the files will get lost, pronto."

"I can't," she said. "Judge Soren—"

The helicopter roared overhead again.

"Now, Louise," I yelled. "Before they block the gate."

She turned to the bacon-headed kid. "Johnnie, you need to go with Mr. Spinning here."

Johnnie smiled even bigger, showing pale, pointed teeth. Then he took my cat Sammy, lifted the animal to his mouth, and swallowed him whole, in one big swoop like the kid's jaw had dislocated. It made my head ache just to see him do it.

Well, then there was a whole lot of commotion, with me throwing up and Louise shouting and the kids running around screaming and the FBI bashing in the front door and waving automatic weapons all over the place.

I'd like to say I kept my head, but there's a lot of things I'd like in this life I ain't never going to get. Next thing I knew, my cheek was pressed into the Persian rug in the living room, with busted crystal cutting into it, while some FBI gorilla in a windbreaker looped my wrists together with cable ties. My knuckles ached something fierce, and someone in the kitchen was cussing a blue streak.

The agent leaned over and breathed hot across the side of my face. Mexican for lunch was my guess. "Where's the kid?" he asked, grabbing my hair and yanking my head back for emphasis.

"What kid?"

Our conversation didn't get any more productive over time, I can tell you.

#

No, the bacon-headed kid never did turn up again. I don't know what happened to him, not for sure. A person could take a guess.

Oh look, it's the cat.

Hey, hey, you can get down off the counter. It's just the cat, for Pete's sake. He does kind of sneak up on a body sometimes.

Yeah, I *know* how big he is. Those little purple-tipped knobs sure are cute, aren't they? Set off the green fur real nice. He's a sweetheart, no trouble at all. Give him a scritch.

See, I knew you'd agree with me. Everybody sees things Sammy's way, once they meet him.

Speak of the devil, there's Louise now. Kids and all, I'm sure. Mama she truck. Reckon I'd better open the store again. You going to clean up that beer you spilled?

Oh, and welcome to our little corner of Texas.

PAX AGRICOLA

Joe Radford heard the bellow of a goat just outside his ancient Airstream trailer. Decades of experience told him what that particular call meant—a proud goat, somewhere she shouldn't be. Joe jumped up from the kitchen table, scattering the spring seed packets he'd just gotten in the mail.

He ran outside to see Bella, the beautiful brown Nubian who was his oldest doe, in the garden nosing at the last of his winter vegetables. Joe's other two goats explored the driveway. It was time to change the latch on the goat pen again—their tongues were like thumbs, and patient as sin. He grabbed a spatula rusting in the grass along with a stray trash can lid and banged them together. "Come on, girls!" he shouted. "Back in the pen."

The two in the driveway, Cloris and Rosaline, scuttled nervously toward their familiar barnyard. Bella gave him a baleful yellow-eyed glare, and bent to the butternut squash. Joe shooed the other two goats all the way in, and with a sigh of despair for his squash, stopped to chain the gate shut.

He left the lid and spatula behind—the racket wouldn't impress Bella, she was too smart for that—and stalked into the garden. She'd knocked the wooden garden gate right off its hinges, and tore the chicken wire away with it. "Come on, girl," Joe said, making little clucking noises. He smiled in spite of the damage to his vegetables. Bella was eating weeks' worth of his meals, but damn was she smart.

The goat suddenly staggered and collapsed against the half-buried gopher fence lining the squash row. A second later, Joe heard the flat crack of a rifle shot. Stumbling through his Vietnam-honed reflex of hitting the dirt, Joe ran to Bella. "God damned morons with hunting rifles," he muttered as he slid to his knees to calm the goat, who bleated softly. Logic told him there wouldn't be a second shot from a flustered hunter, but his back still had that target itch.

Bella had taken the bullet in the shoulder. Her flesh wasn't badly torn, but the real damage would be inside. Joe took her jaw in his hand, stared at the barred pupils of her golden eyes. She glared back at him, angry and ornery as ever, her musky goat smell mixed with hot tang of blood. This goat wasn't going to die, not in the next few minutes anyway. She was too pissed for that. Joe took off his second-best work shirt, tore it in half and knotted the sleeve ends together to wind the rags around Bella's shoulder and across her chest as a simple pressure bandage.

Half naked and daubed with the goat's blood, Joe trotted toward the wooded fence line separating his property from Ralph Farney's just to the west—a deer-and-quail hunting lease. By the time he got to the barbed wire, a big red SUV was slewing down Ralph's access road, too fast for Joe to get the plates.

Late February was out of season for deer anyway, so the idiot had to have been hunting on a quail license. Couldn't resist that big brown doe glimpsed through the trees, no doubt. By sundown, the son of a bitch who fired the shot would have his old frat brothers swearing he had been at the golf course with them all day. Joe knew from long experience that Ralph would be ignorant of any wrongdoing. Ralph made too much money off dumb-assed Austin lawyers to turn any of them in for a little violation like this. The income made Ralph stupid, which pissed Joe off. He firmly believed that a little strife was good for the soul—damn it, he liked cranky neighbors, they left him alone—but this was ridiculous.

Back in the garden Bella struggled to her feet. Helping her, Joe knew he should have the goat put down and slaughtered, which would provide food for almost a whole season, but Bella was too good a friend to treat that way. So he got the last of the month's cash out of the coffee can under the trailer's hitch, evicted some chickens to load Bella into the back seat of his rusty white Gran Torino station wagon, and headed into Lockhart to see the large animal vet.

#

Back from the vet, tired and flat broke, Joe knelt in the garden in the cool orange light of dusk and looked at the seeds he'd rescued from the kitchen floor. Each spring he got his order from some hippies out west. Near as he could tell from the little catalog, they were a bunch of tie-dyed fruitcakes living in old school buses, but they had the best damned tomato seeds going, and some mighty fine cucumbers and squash as well.

Just like every year, the packets were handmade from recycled paper grocery bags and sealed with wax, the varieties stamped on them with fanciful lettering in spotty, colored ink. This time he'd got in Moreton and Carnival tomatoes, Gold Rush zucchini, Saladin cucumbers for his pickles, and just because he liked the name, Jack of Hearts watermelons. Rifling through the bucket he'd put the seed packets in, Joe found the usual scribbled invoice, this year with a note clipped to it:

Dear Mr. Radford. Because you are such a loyal customer, we have enclosed a special gift. Yours in Green Earth, South Cascade Seeds.

And those Oregon hippies had sent him a new variety, their gift from the Pacific Northwest. Joe almost smiled. The kraft paper packet just read "Pax Agricola"—probably one of them Latin names the nurserymen used—with two little girl fairies kissing over a flower Joe couldn't identify. Right below that, someone had written "Water with love."

Water with love. Right. Singing Grateful Dead tunes the whole time, probably. Love or no love, Joe doubted this whatever-it-was would even grow in Central Texas so far out of Oregon's cold and damp, but what the heck? He'd planted worse, and he could always turn the row over for a summer vegetable if the pax agricola didn't grow.

Joe needed to work dirt, to forget the idiots on Ralph's lease and his worries about Bella's wound getting infected. There weren't any directions on the packet, so Joe turned the soil in one of the rows he'd left fallow for the winter and mixed in bone meal and manure. With a gardener's natural economy he shook out half the seeds, inspecting their hulls. Finally, by the early moonlight he planted them one by one, each slipping beneath the earth as delicate as a kiss.

#

The pax agricola sprouted almost overnight, fast as anything he'd ever seen, sending up the hopeful green swords of little shoots. Joe studied them, trying to determine if they were vines, or bushes, or what. From the little stamp on the packet, he had imagined a tall plant, like a Kansas sunflower, but of course there was no telling yet.

That day he mulched the shoots carefully against a possible late frost and double-checked his repairs to the goat-damaged chicken wire and the gopher fence.

#

Saturday night Ralph Farney's older boy Willie Ed, a varsity forward for the Lockhart Lions basketball team, brought several of his buddies and a couple of girls onto the deer lease. Joe watched the bonfire gleam through the woods for a while, until the shrieking started. He tried to call the sheriff on the party line, but Agnes Delore was badmouthing the other ladies in the Emmanuel Episcopal altar guild in great detail and pretended not to hear him asking her to get off the phone. So Joe walked to the fence and climbed over.

"What are you kids doin'?" he shouted into the glare of the bonfire.

Willie Ed was lying down in a clinch with some girl Joe didn't recognize, one hand inside her sweater, the other down the waistband of her jeans. Another boy hung back. All three stared at Joe.

"Get out of here, old man," Willie Ed said in a rough voice that probably scared the freshman back at Lockhart High.

Joe folded his arms. "Somebody screamed."

The girl glanced into the darkness on the other side of the fire as the second boy grabbed a burning branch. "He said get out," the other boy shouted, waving the stick.

"Where is she?" Joe asked the girl, ignoring the boys.

"Willie Ed," she said, pushing her boyfriend off. "We should go." The girl started to wiggle away. "I'm getting Nancy."

"Stupid old turd," Willie Ed said to Joe with a snarl, then turned away.

A minute later, Joe watched two more boys and another girl walk out of the shadows beyond the fire. The six kids got into a minivan and drive off. The other girl—Nancy?—was crying, but there wasn't much he could do about that. At least he'd got them to stop messing with her. Maybe she'd learned something.

The next morning his gate was bashed in and his mailbox was missing, the post a splintered stump.

"Farney's kid?" said the Caldwell County sheriff's deputy who answered the phone. "Hmm . . . Well, that's a problem now, isn't it?"

Joe knew where this was going, but he had to try. "That's what I thought," he said. "Kid's a problem."

The deputy sighed. "Think about it some more, Joe. The basketball team's going to the Division II playoffs. School really needs him. Lot of people will be angry if he's in trouble. Look, don't rock the boat. My advice is work it out quietly with Ralph."

Joe hung up on the deputy. Sometimes there was no point.

#

A couple of weeks later, getting on into March, the pax agricola plants were pretty—long, leggy stems, purple-edged leaves like little blades, and already a puffy crown like Queen Anne's lace got before it flowered and bolted to seed. They were only a couple of feet tall, but Joe figured they'd hit five or six feet full-grown.

He spent a quiet Tuesday afternoon raising the chicken wire higher above the pax agricola and weeding out the Johnson grass in his garden rows. The garden was more peaceful and satisfying this spring, somehow. Bella's stitches were healing up clean, so Joe had set aside the antibiotics for future use. The chickens clucked quietly in the yard around the trailer and the turkey vultures circled high overhead in a blue silk sky. It was a perfect Texas spring day.

#

Joe's wife called him that night.

"What the hell are you doing?" Beth Ann demanded as soon as he picked up the phone.

"Hello, honey," Joe said. "Nice to hear your voice again."

"Don't you *honey* me, you white trash fool. I haven't seen a check in three months. Only reason you don't have a demand letter from Pettigrew already is he said I had to call you first."

Just like old times, Beth Ann riding his ass from the first flap of her gums. Also just like old times, she was full of it. As Joe understood the concept, "temporary support" was supposed to run out eventually, but he and Beth Ann had been in the process of getting divorced for almost six years. Pettigrew, her boyfriend-attorney, had a buddy in the family court in Travis County, and somehow things never turned out like Joe expected, what with the endless stream of continuances, stays and refilings. Stuffed behind the paneled walls of his trailer, all that paperwork made nice insulation.

Joe was pretty sure the system wasn't supposed to work this way, but he didn't know who to complain to, and he didn't have the money for his own lawyer. Besides, all the legal fuss kept his wife away from him, which was the real point.

"Beth Ann," Joe said into the tense silence on the line, "You haven't had a check because Pettigrew attached my pension last fall. If I work to make enough money to pay you, I'll lose my Social Security, too. Then I'll have nothing."

"Joe," she said, her voice growing sharper, "a woman has needs. Just because you're lazy doesn't mean I should do without."

Last time he'd seen Beth Ann, she was driving Pettigrew's fancy German car. "I understand about needs, honey," he said, trying to be reasonable.

"Well, you *need* to send me some money, or I'll *need* to have you back in court. And Pettigrew says you won't like it this time."

Joe hadn't liked it the last few times, either. But the alternatives were worse. For one thing, if he didn't give her some money, she might come out here and visit him. "In the mail tomorrow," he said.

Beth Ann hung up on him. Joe sighed, then went out to his coffee can under the trailer hitch. He had just cashed this month's social security check. It was a hell of a price to pay, but at least he had his garden, and his solitude.

#

One Sunday morning a few weeks later, the pax agricola bloomed. They had matured much faster than Joe had expected. It was only late March, and great purple-and-yellow flowers were bursting from the tall plants, each as high as his head.

The blossoms were narrow, like lilies, but more open, with variegated petals and the dusty smell of summer in their fragrance. As he sniffed them, Joe was reminded of the endless summers of his long-ago youth, chasing snakes in the tall grass, and nights between the cool sheets, savoring a chocolate bar snuck into bed.

He liked the smell so much that he fetched a pitcher of tea and his lone dinette chair and made a place in the garden where he could sit and watch the flowers. Each bloom was its own miracle, each plant its own world. This was why Joe lived in the country, put up with the inconveniences and indignities of his life. The glory of nature, brought forth by his green thumb, sunlight and water.

There was plenty to be done around the place, but the plants were too nice. Joe didn't usually find himself being so lazy on a good working day, but somehow this felt right.

"Howdy, Mr. Radford," said a young man.

Looking up, Joe recognized the newcomer as the kid who'd threatened him with the burning branch. "Yeah?"

"It's, uh, me. Tony Alvarez. You remember?"

"I remember. Can I help you?" Joe was surprised at himself as soon as he said it—normally he would have run the punk right off.

"Thought I'd fix up that busted gate a little more, then come sit with you a while here in the garden." The kid looked at his feet. Joe could swear Tony was blushing. "If you don't mind. Seeing as I owe you an apology and all."

"I guess so," said Joe. "I believe there's another chair in the hayloft of the goat barn." He really didn't care for visitors, but the kid seemed okay.

A little while later a red SUV came crunching down the gravel drive and parked next to Joe's old Ford. Three young men in suits and ties got out. Two of them walked over to the goat pen while the third brought Joe a big sack.

"Got some burritos on the way down here," the man explained with a grin. "Mind if we visit a while? We, uh, kind of want to make up for Decker over there being such an idiot." The stranger nodded toward the goat pen, where his two friends were feeding carrots to Bella, Cloris and Rosaline.

Joe's face felt prickly, hot, like he was embarrassed, but he wasn't. He rarely felt that way, and certainly not now. What was happening? He glanced at the flowering pax agricola. They nodded gently in the breeze.

Then Joe realized there wasn't a breeze blowing. "Suit yourself," he said, almost straining against his own words, "but I've about run out of chairs." Two was his limit, for all kinds of good reasons.

The man smiled. "We brought our own gear." Then, as he turned away, he added, "And, hey . . . thanks for letting everything be okay."

By noon, all the kids from the bonfire had shown up. The basketball players were fixing the windows on Joe's old trailer, caulking them tight, while the high school girls and the lawyers cleaned up inside. Ralph Farney and Agnes Delore came around with shovels and a wheelbarrow and cleaned out the goat barn, while two sheriff's deputies parked their cruiser in the driveway and in no time had the carburetor of the Gran Torino spread out on a towel, rebuilding it from a kit they'd bought in town. Even Gracie Thompson, the rural letter carrier that serviced Joe's R.F.D, turned up on her own time, hand-delivering a large check from social security making up for a long-term shortfall in their calculations of Joe's benefits. Gracie stayed to cook lunch for everyone on Joe's little smoker—sausages and potatoes she'd brought with her.

There were too many people, acting too nice, trampling all over his land, and somehow it just didn't matter. Joe tried real hard to think about that, but every time he concentrated on his irritation, it slipped away from him. He had the overwhelming sensation that life was good, life was supposed to be good, and that he shouldn't worry about it.

That scared the hell out of him.

Fear cleared his thinking. It had to be the damned pax agricola flowers. Everything that normally went wrong around him was suddenly too right. *That* meant Beth Ann and Pettigrew would be here soon. He really didn't want to see his wife. Magic flowers or not, she was out of his life and he liked it that way. No way was he reconciling under the influence of pax agricola. Not with her, not with Ralph Farney, not with no one.

He stood up, reached for one of the pax agricola flowers, to see if he could break it off the stem. It was like reaching into mud—his hand moved slower and slower the closer it got to the flower. Joe got the feeling he could spend the rest of his life reaching for that flower and still never touch it.

Behind him, the double-toned blare of Pettigrew's car horn echoed through the woods along the driveway. Joe turned to see the red BMW pull to a stop behind the parked sheriff's cruiser. Following the BMW was a parade of vehicles, filled with people he vaguely recognized—court clerks and Wal-Mart cashiers—and plenty more he didn't. A helicopter clattered overhead, then banked over the second-growth woods to look for an open field in which to land.

"Holy shit," Joe whispered.

"All these people coming together and helping out . . . it's like the beginning of peace, Mr. Radford," said Tony Alvarez.

Joe didn't want peace, he wanted solitude, damn it. If he didn't do something quick, Beth Ann would be all over him trying to make up, and Joe would *never* be ready for that. If the problem was in the garden, well, there was a solution for gardens. "I'm getting my goat," said Joe. He shouldered Tony out of the way, marched to the goat pen, and whistled for Bella.

The old brown nanny wandered up, glaring at him as usual. The liquid gold eyes with their barred pupils could be unsettling to people who didn't know goats, but Joe and Bella understood one another. He undid the latch, put one hand on her collar and stroked her neck with the other. "I've got a special treat for you, girl," Joe whispered in her ear. "You'll love this. We're going to the *garden*."

All the years Joe had spent keeping the goats out of the garden had certainly taught Bella that word. She bleated, pulling him along to the chicken wire gate. Joe let the goat in, led her along the rows of sprouting zucchini, cucumber and watermelon, and stopped in front of the pax agricola. "I can't touch 'em," he whispered in Bella's ear, "but you're ornery enough to eat damned near anything, so do the right thing, old girl. Give me my life back."

Tony Alvarez gave Joe a puzzled look. "You're letting the goat into the garden?"

Bella sniffed the thick stalk of one of the pax agricola.

"Yep," said Joe, "and not a moment too soon."

In the distance he heard Beth Ann calling his name.

"Bella, just do it," Joe said. Fine time for the goat to develop some manners.

"Hey, that goat, she's—" Tony was interrupted by Joe putting a hand over his mouth.

"Never you mind, boy," said Joe. Bella munched the first stalk. The flower collapsed in a spray of purple-and-yellow pollen. "Things can be too easy, sometimes."

The goat set to the pax agricola with an appetite. She chewed down

131

the stalks, ate the blooms, tore the leaves. As Bella finished off the plants, the hum of work around his little farm settled down to an uneasy calm.

"Well, Joe," said Beth Ann as she stepped into the garden.

"Hello, honey," said Joe. She was the same as ever—peroxide hair, leopardskin spandex, a leather miniskirt. It didn't look as good on her as it had thirty-five years and forty pounds ago. Just the sight of her was irritating. Then voices began to rise again, this time in anger—arguments breaking out, shouts, curses, all the ragged symphony of daily life.

Beth Ann's voice was just as nasty as the rest. "This is about normal for you. You can screw up anything."

Over her shoulder, Joe could see the deputies slugging it out with one of the Austin lawyers. Pettigrew stalked toward Joe with an angry look in his eye.

"I think it's the end of peace now, Mr. Radford," said Tony.

As the goat started in on the zucchini seedlings, Joe smiled. "Back to normal. Ain't it great?"

#

After the County Attorney decided there wasn't any point in prosecution for incitement to riot and disturbing the peace, Joe got out of jail and came home to find that Agnes Delore and Tony Alvarez had been feeding his goats and keeping an eye on the garden. Tony told him the goats had behaved. The Gran Torino really did run better, and the trailer was less drafty, so the whole sorry business hadn't been a total loss.

Joe sat at the little table, examining the kraft paper pax agricola packet. He tipped a few of the remaining seeds into his hand. Tiny things, to do so much, he thought, rolling them back and forth with his fingertip. He wondered for a moment how they'd taste. "You never know," Joe said aloud, then dropped the seeds back into the packet and reached for the tape to seal it up. Maybe next year he'd be ready for more peace and less quiet.

Outside, a goat bellowed. It didn't sound like one of his. Uh-oh, thought Joe. He peeked out the trailer's tiny window toward the goat barn and the pen surrounding it. . . . Bella leaned against the gatepost, scratching herself and glaring at him as she chewed her cud. Then Joe saw a whole parade of goats picking their way on to his property, heading for the pen.

GRATITUDE

That corkscrew thing came wiggling across the sky like a drunk home-coming queen. Me and Billy Ralph McMahon was out poaching jackrabbits near Saint Johns Colony when it thundered over our heads.

"Gabriel's a-coming!" Billy Ralph screamed as he threw his shotgun into the bushes and dropped to his knees.

The blast damn near parted my hair two inches deep. "What the hell are you doing?"

"I ain't going to face Judgment with no gun in my hands," Billy Ralph said. His voice was all quivery.

"Oh, shut up," I said. "That weren't no angel, you cottonhead, that was an airplane."

Then the ground shook, pebbles jumping as the mesquite trees swayed.

"An airplane that just crashed," I added.

We fished Billy Ralph's shotgun out of the sage and got into my truck, my late Pappy's old 1958 International with the bad cylinder head. I couldn't get the truck past forty no matter what, so it took us a while to find that thing, even being in a hurry. Someday I'll get me a better one.

Someday.

#

Heading down 812 toward Red Rock, we found the airplane stuck in the ground near the railroad tracks. There weren't nobody there except a Bastrop County sheriff's deputy, afraid to get out of his car. Me and Billy Ralph jumped out of the truck and climbed the fence.

We couldn't get too close to the thing. Even though I couldn't quite see it, I could tell it was huge, taller than a water tower. I swear up in the sky it was shaped like a corkscrew or a coil spring, but here stuck point-down into the ground it mostly looked like quivery air. Like to make me sick at my stomach to get too near.

Half a dozen Brangus cows in the field with that thing was laying down, legs splayed out. It was a killer. But the weirdest part was the grass around that killer airplane had been turned to crystal. I could see the stalks already busting under their own weight.

"Get down," shouted Billy Ralph. He fired his shotgun past my shoulder at something scuttling through the weeds.

My ears rang so bad I couldn't hear myself cuss, so I didn't bother. Instead I took off after whatever he'd seen.

Billy Ralph may not of had the brains God gave a goose, but he hits what he shoots at. This blessed thing was about three feet tall, silver, with glossy black eyes and steaming purple blood. It was naked and didn't have no tackle between its legs.

In fact, it looked just like one of them space aliens the National Enquirer was always showing meeting the Queen of England or whoever.

"Damn," said Billy Ralph. His voice was real tiny, like down a well, which meant my hearing was coming back already. "My sister was right."

I looked back over at the deputy sheriff. He was out of his car, talking to a state trooper that had just pulled up, and pointing at us. "Time for us to go," I shouted.

We walked back across the field, smiling at the cops and shrugging. As we climbed the fence, I saw the grass rippling along the railroad tracks on the far side of the alien spaceship. Then dozens of little silver guys hustled over the tracks and into the mesquite.

"Well, shit fire," I muttered.

#

After hassling us for about five minutes, the cops got distracted when the National Guard choppers came roaring overhead. I guess they didn't realize we'd actually killed one of the little beggars, or they'd of arrested us on the spot. So we split when the choppers started touching down.

Going back down County Road 61, we found a school bus slewed over in the ditch. High school kids leaned out the windows, hootin' and hollerin' for serious.

"Looks like trouble," I said to Billy Ralph as I grabbed my Colt King Cobra .357 out of the glove box and jumped out. Billy Ralph bailed out the other side with his shotgun.

"What's up?" I yelled at Lovely Mullins, who was hanging her big chest out the window at me.

"Aliens eating the bus!" she shouted back at me.

I ran around to the ditch. The front end of the bus was down in there, with four or five of them little aliens crowding around it. Margie Estrada, the driver, was whacking at them with her tire pressure rod. They ignored her as they chewed on the front left tire.

"Get back, Margie!" I yelled.

Then I walked up and popped them, one, two, three, four, with the pistol. I could hear smacking under the hood, so I dropped to the grass in the purple blood. There was two more under the hood, working on the radiator hose. I rolled away fast afore the hose busted. The aliens screeched and scuttled out, running away from the boiling stuff. Billy Ralph put them out of our misery.

"Damn," we both said as the kids on the bus screamed even louder.

Then I heard a siren. At least this was self-defense. I figured I could talk our way out of it.

#

Turns out discharging firearms in the presence of school children, even in a good cause, is damn near a felony. What the hell has Texas come to?

"It's very lucky we found you," said the doc. He was a little character in a tweed suit with big glasses, out riding shotgun with one of the deputies. Far as I could tell, he was the reason we hadn't been arrested yet, this go round. "You and Mr. McMahon are the best informants we have so far."

"Whoa, wait up, doc," I said, stepping away from him with my hands up between us. "I ain't no rat."

The doc chuckled. "You misunderstand me, sir. I mean you have had the most experience with our visitors."

"Yeah, we *killed* 'em," muttered Billy Ralph.

"It's a mistake." The doc shook his head. "It has to be. At least, it was a terrible misfortune that our first visitors from the stars mistook a school bus for a threatening target."

"Threatening?" I couldn't believe my ears. "Threatening? They wasn't attacking it, they was eating it!"

"It's a communication problem," the doc explained patiently. "We've got to figure out how to talk to them."

"Sooner talk to roaches," said Billy Ralph.

Roaches, I thought. Was they just roaches?

#

When we finally got home about four in the afternoon, Pappy's old truck had taken up a new noise. I figured it was like to throw a rod.

"Well, hell," I sighed as I got out of the truck. Something new I didn't have the cash or the tools to fix. "For another day." I threw the doc's papers and business card in my burn barrel. "Them aliens . . . why would they be after tires and antifreeze? Tires is made of rubber, and antifreeze is alcohol and chemicals."

"Everything under a bus's got grease on it," said Billy Ralph.

"By God, Billy Ralph, sometimes a body might even think you've got brains in that head of yours. Grease."

I ran into the chicken coop and found a two-gallon can of axle grease. I lugged it back outside. "They wasn't after antifreeze. They was chewing the grease off the hose lines. Just like roaches, eatin' their way across the county instead of across my kitchen." I grinned at him. "Let's catch us an alien cockroach."

I spread the grease all up and down an old one-by-twelve, which I laid in the middle of the driveway in front of my trailer house. Billy Ralph worked his way back up toward the county road, daubing grease on the gravel every couple of steps with an old paintbrush while I hoisted some ammo into our deer blind in the big pecan tree by the corral gate.

It wasn't twenty minutes later when another one of those little silver beggars come down the driveway, slurping up that axle grease. Me and Billy Ralph was in the deer blind, locked and loaded. The thing ran right up to our one-by-twelve and commenced to bogart the grease like there weren't no tomorrow. We wasted him, purple blood everywhere.

"Proof is in the pudding," I said.

I thought about how many there was. We'd seen maybe two dozen, accounted for eight. No reason there couldn't of been a hundred more, not out in that field near Red Rock. And there weren't no way two fellers with guns could handle that many.

But there was other ways to do it.

I took a deep breath. "Billy Ralph . . . I need your Momma's wood chipper."

"No way, Lamar," he said. "You ain't never brung back my uncle's bass boat."

He was such an idiot. "*You* sank it, remember?"

Billy Ralph got that little whine in his voice. "Yeah, but *you* borrowed it."

"I don't want to talk about that damned boat. I need the wood chipper." I thought about that doc and them National Guard troops. What if the little silver beggars started eating the hoses off the helicopters? "It's a matter of national security."

"Uh-huh."

"Plus I'll tell Mabel about you getting that waitress's phone number out in Elgin."

"I'll be right back," he said, climbing out of the deer blind and heading for his Ford flatbed.

"Axle grease," I yelled after him. "Go to Wal-Mart and NAPA and get all the axle grease you can find."

He waved as his truck lurched up the driveway.

#

While Billy Ralph was gone, I built a ramp, kind of like what them trick water skiers use at Sea World, up about six feet with a little flat ledge at the top. Then I got some beer out of the cooler and waited.

He didn't get back with the wood chipper until near about sundown. He had two fifty-five gallon drums on the flatbed, along with some boxes with cans of axle grease sticking out of them.

"What took you so long?" I said.

Billy Ralph jumped out of his truck. "God damned National Guard has Lockhart about shut down. They're asking questions everywhere, looking for them little silver stinkers. Doc still wants to talk to them."

"Sooner talk to the roaches. Help me get that chipper over here."

We unhooked it from the Ford and wrestled it into place next to the ramp I'd built. The chipper's intake was about two feet below the ramp's ledge. Perfect. I laid a couple of sections of one-by-twelve slanting downward from the ledge to the intake and duct taped them in place.

"What the hell?" asked Billy Ralph.

"Axle grease," I told him. "We slather it all over these boards leading into the intake, then daub it back out to the road like before. Maybe spill a bunch by the front gate. Lash one of them fifty-fives sideways with a little cock valve, you could spread grease all the way to Red Rock. They follow it here, on up the ramp, see that mother lode—bingo. Axle grease is slippery as hell, they'll slide into that wood chipper smooth as goat shit."

Billy Ralph chewed that one over. "What are you going to do while I spread grease from here to Red Rock?"

"Hide in the chicken coop and run out from time to time to keep grease spread on that last bit of ramp. And keep the chipper fueled if need be."

"Roaches, huh? Lot of trouble for some alien bugs."

#

Billy Ralph hadn't come back yet when they started boiling down the driveway around full dark. Them little beggars was everywhere. Right down the driveway, up the ramp, dive onto the grease, and into the chipper.

By the moonlight I could see the chipper spraying purple shit all over the yard and across the front of my trailer house. There was dozens of 'em, maybe hundreds, shoving onto my ramp three and five at a time.

I hadn't counted on my alien trap working this well. I jumped on top of the chicken coop to get clear, because they'd started to fight amongst themselves.

Then the bull alien showed up.

There I was on top of my coop, aliens the size of dogs throwing themselves into my wood chipper, and this thing towering over me. Behind it I saw the running lights of helicopters. The National Guard was after this one. This one was after me.

"Crap," I whispered. I didn't even bother to go for the .357.

It was about twenty-five feet tall, kind of a long, stretchy version of those little ones that had been deviling the county all afternoon. The bull alien looked skinnier than I would of expected for its size, but was hard to tell for sure in the dark, with the glare from the helicopter searchlights wobbling through the sky. The bull alien's big gleaming eyes were slanted just like the little ones. It came to a stop, one giant foot stomping the cab of Pappy's truck flat, and stared at me.

"Well, hell," I said. I stood up on the roof of the coop. If I was going to die with Pappy's truck, I was going to die on my feet.

"You," it said, in a voice like a giant, rusted hinge.

"Me?"

More of the little alien pests swarmed around the bull alien's big, flat feet. It raised one leg and stomped about a dozen of them into grape jelly.

"Exterminator?" the bull alien asked.

"No," I squeaked. "Country boy."

Off to my left, Billy Ralph tore into the yard in the Ford flatbed, horn beeping. The helicopters circled close. I realized that Billy Ralph was pulling a wide turn through the tomato patch to make a run at the bull alien's legs.

And this thing probably wasn't gonna kill me, 'cause it would of done it already. "Damn, Billy Ralph, you sure picked a bad time to grow a set of balls," I whispered.

"Gratitude," the bull alien creaked.

I whipped the pistol out of my belt and shot out the front tires of Billy Ralph's truck. Billy Ralph right near clipped his Momma's wood chipper as he swerved into the chicken coop where I was standing.

The coop exploded into a cloud of glass, metal, wood, feathers and angry chickens. I went ass over teakettle to wind up in the bed of Pappy's truck, right between the feet of the bull alien. Glass punched into my elbows.

"Pests," it said, then lumbered off into the darkness.

A helicopter landed in the ruined tomato patch about the same time Billy Ralph fought his way out of a cloud of angry chickens and squealing aliens. The next thing I knew I was face down the muzzle of an M-16 against my head and a boot in the middle of my back. Billy Ralph was next to me in the same position, rolling his eyes and crying.

Whatever was going to happen next didn't on account of that corkscrew went flaming through the sky.

"I reckon they're gone," I said as we all looked up—me, Billy Ralph, the National Guardsmen. "Just left them little silver roaches behind."

#

After the corkscrew ship left, the soldiers tried to round up the last of the little aliens. They mostly scrapped and fought and found their way into the wood chipper before some sergeant thought to shut it off.

Then there was a lot of shouting, and threatening, and some legal stuff to sign—"non-disclosures" and "indemnifications." But by dawn, it was just me and Billy Ralph in the wreckage of my place.

"We're out two trucks, your tomato patch and your hen house," said Billy Ralph.

"Still got the wood chipper," I said.

"Yeah, but there's purple shit all over your trailer."

"Well, hell," I said. "God damned aliens messed everything up."

We wandered over to my truck, which looked like a Twinkie that had met with a ball peen hammer.

"Your Pappy sure would be disappointed in this," Billy Ralph said.

"Engine was going anyway." I raised the hood, which was sprung loose from the alien-stomping the truck had received.

Billy Ralph leaned over the fender with me. Underneath the grease and dirt and duct tape, the engine gleamed.

"Damn," said Billy Ralph. "It never looked like that before."

That bull alien had changed the entire God damned engine block to gold, along with anything else made of iron or steel under that hood.

"A new truck," I said. I could feel my lungs filling up for a great big whoop. "And a new bass boat!" I hollered loud enough to scare the chickens all over again. "And I'm going to get me a doublewide!"

"Hot damn," said Billy Ralph. "Saved the world and got us a tip, too."

HITCHING TO AURORA

The reds were the worst. The blue ones just died on the hood. The reds streaked from the sunny August sky to explode on the windshield like jello-filled balloons. Ross had the wipers running, in case they were real. On the seat next to him, the raccoon screamed over the blasting Southern-fried rock and hurled itself against the rusted wire of its cage.

Farm Road 730 was two lanes of hot Texas blacktop heading due north across the Wise County line to Aurora. To be up for the trip, Ross had fortified himself with two gel caps of psilocybin spores. He had more as needed. He sipped from a fifth of Jaegermeister, keeping things going in the right direction.

Big Tolliver had called last night and told Ross to meet him at the cemetery in Aurora. Or else. Big Tolliver wanted to discuss Ross's debts. All Ross had was his car—a 1970 Chrysler New Yorker older than he was, with a blown hemi under a cutout hood, glass-packed side pipes, and treaded drag slicks. It was worth about ten grand. He hoped Big Tolliver would call things settled with the gift of the car. Ross wanted out of dealing, finally. But if things didn't work out, he had other options.

The raccoon was one of those options. So were the rabbits in the trunk. Ross had forty pounds of ice back there to keep them cool, and his brother's shotgun just in case things got out of hand. He'd had a plan last night when he'd broken into Animal Control, right after Big

Tolliver called. Was it rabies? Ross took another sip of Jaeger to fortify his thinking.

Trailing bright smears, a big red one bounced into the middle of the road. Ross swerved hard to the left, crossing the centerline and onto the oncoming shoulder, careful not to spill his booze. With the Jaeger making his eyes blurry Ross couldn't quite read the speedometer, but he thought he was pushing forty. That seemed plenty fast, even though the car wanted to do more like one-forty. Ross usually did too when sober, but he'd been driving with one foot on the brake all afternoon for fear of the reds and blues. And the damned raccoon wouldn't shut up.

Ross recrossed the centerline to a blaring horn and shrieking tires. He gave the other driver the finger. "Son of a bitch's lucky the shotgun's in the trunk," Ross told the raccoon. The Chrysler lurched onto the left shoulder in a spray of gravel, momentarily overwhelming his ability to both think and drive. As Ross recovered, he noticed a dwarf by the side of the road up ahead.

Ross banged on the raccoon's cage, setting off another round of screeching. "Check out the little dude hitchhiking." The raccoon spit at him. "I *think* he's real," Ross added.

Through a color-streaked haze, he could see it was a kid wearing a Nomex suit, like a NASCAR driver without any patches. "He shouldn't be out here by himself," Ross told the raccoon. He took another sip of Jaeger, just for luck.

The raccoon hurled itself against the wire, bouncing the cage against the dash.

The road seemed momentarily free of red and blue ones, so Ross pulled over, trying not to cream the little dude. Risking the loss of several fingers, he tugged the cage out of the way, then pulled the door handle.

Wiping raccoon spittle from his ear, Ross shouted, "Hop in, little dude. You okay?"

"I am <click> fine, well, excellent," the kid said. . . . The kid's voice was weird, like he talked from inside an empty septic tank. Strangely, Ross didn't have any trouble hearing the hollow little voice over Ronnie Van Zandt's wailing and the chest-shaking rumble of the car.

As the kid climbed in, Ross could see he had a huge head. Either that, or the kid was wearing a space alien mask. Ross couldn't quite tell, what with the Jaeger and the mushroom spores. Big slanted eyes gleamed dark in a little face—over it all the kid wore a silver suit with silver gear on a belt. Must be a Japanese tourist. The raccoon was suddenly real quiet.

"Um. Okay." Ross tried again, yelling over the Skynyrd, which he turned down to merely deafening. "Where you headed?"

"<click> Thirty-three degrees, four minutes, north, ninety-seven degrees, thirty minutes, west, City of Aurora, Wise County, State of Texas, United States of America, North America, Earth, Solar System, Western Spiral Arm."

Ross really missed the reds and blues. Them he understood. He took another sip of Jaeger as a conversational aid. "Right. Aurora. It's your lucky day, kid, that's where I'm heading. Did you know there's a space alien buried there? Close the door."

"My <click> friends, associates, crewmates must join me."

"Uh . . . okay." Ross couldn't figure what to say as six more of the little silver dudes popped out of the sage by the shoulder of the road. Running around like scattered chickens, they tried to climb into the car all at once, accompanied by clicks and whistles. Two of them knocked each other down, as a third clambered past them into the car, sliding right over the top of the front seat. The others followed in a tumble, one kicking the volume of the stereo all the way down while another knocked the Jaegermeister over. Liquor oozed over the seat.

"Crap!" Ross yelled. "Not the stereo. And *way* not the booze."

The first kid picked up the bottle. "Our <click> apologies, regrets, condolences. Allow me to make <click> amends, restitution, compensation." He stuck one silver finger into the bottle, which filled with dark fluid. The spreading pool on the seat diminished, but even after it disappeared the kid kept going to top off the bottle. He licked his finger and offered the liquor to Ross.

"Whoa, dude, that was a hell of a trick," Ross said. He sniffed the proffered booze. "That's Jaeger, alright." After taking a slug, he grinned at the kids in back. Each of them carried a collection of metallic silver gear, like Boy Scouts who had wandered through a paint booth. They all looked exactly the same. The hair on his arms prickled as the first kid pulled the door shut.

"Right," Ross said, waving the newly-filled bottle. Spitting gravel, the New Yorker pulled back onto the highway. Ross kept it slow, in case of red and blue ones. He didn't think the 'shroom spores were having much effect, but seven identical silver twins didn't seem right. Maybe he needed more Jaeger.

#

A couple of miles later Ross slipped Molly Hatchet into the CD player. The raccoon had curled into a whimpering ball in the corner of its cage furthest from the new kids. Ross could hear the rabbits thumping loudly in the trunk, pushing to get out. Still keeping his foot close to the brake, Ross let the car get up to forty-five, risking reds and blues to get to Aurora sooner.

He snuck peeks at the little dude in the front seat. The kid sat perfectly still, staring down the highway. Ross's patience broke first. Over Danny Joe Brown's screeching lyrics, he yelled, "I gotta ask, man, why y'all headed to Aurora?"

"We are on a <click> pilgrimage, peregrination, tour." A tuneful chorus of whistling clicks came from the back. "Are you on a similar <click> mission, purpose, goal?"

Ross digested that. "Um, no. Big Tolliver's going to tear me a new one if I don't fork over what I owe him. This car's all I've got to give."

"Are you desiring a new <click> one, thing, individual torn for you?"

Ross slumped down in the seat, accidentally causing the car to accelerate. "Don't want to talk about it."

Whistles and clicks broke out from the back seat. The kid in front whistled a response, then said, "May we share your <click> potable, liquor, drink?"

Ross looked at the newly-refilled bottle. "Hell, it's half yours. Party on, little dudes." He reached over the seat with the Jaegermeister, which was snatched from his hand.

More highway rumbled under the tires of the Chrysler. Ross scanned the low, sunburned hills to each side, watching for reds and blues. He figured he could turn off the wipers now, but he couldn't find the switch. The Jaeger was definitely keeping him loose. Every time there was a gap between songs, he heard the rabbits thumping in the trunk.

"But why Aurora?" he finally asked, rejoining his own conversation. "Ain't nothing there but a couple of churches, a Dairy Queen and a graveyard. There's dead people and ice cream in every town in Texas."

The kid glanced in the back seat before answering. "<click> Graveyard, necropolis, cemetery. That is our <click> mission, purpose, goal."

From the back, an increasingly ragged chorus of whistles and clicks.

"The alien, dude, you're going to see the dead alien in the Aurora cemetery. That's where I'm going. Oh, wow, this is like *Twilight Zone*." A delayed wave of alcohol-fueled paranoia washed over Ross. "You all ain't working for Big Tolliver?"

"No <click> understanding, acquaintance, friendship with Big Tolliver. We seek missing <click> control, opener, keys."

Ross chuckled. "Lost your keys in the cemetery, huh? Must have been some party. Where you all from, anyway?"

Raucous whistles and clicks from the back this time. "Canada," said the kid in the front seat. "We are from <click> Canada, the Northland, the British Commonwealth."

"Oh." Ross was disappointed. Here he had thought they were foreigners, instead of just Yankees. "I had y'all pegged for Japanese boy scouts."

The raccoon whimpered on the floor as Ross swerved to avoid a blue one. To be safe, he slowed down as the nearly-empty Jaegermeister bottle was passed forward from the back. Ross polished it off and tossed the bottle onto the passenger side floor.

#

The New Yorker idled up to the cemetery like a freight train on the prowl. A narrow stone stairway led up an embankment to the grave-yard, passing beneath a white metal arch with black letters reading "AURORA CEMETERY." Scattered post oaks provided indifferent shade. Ross hadn't seen any red or blue ones for a while. The silver kids in the back whistled and clicked like crazy to that really annoying song from *Cats*. Ross had developed a splitting headache.

"Enough show tunes," Ross said. "We're here." Kicking, squirming and tripping over each other, still singing in their whistling clicks, the silver kids bailed out the passenger door, which Ross pulled shut behind them.

He popped the trunk lid from the glove box button, then tugged the raccoon cage out after him on the driver's side, keeping the cage door facing in. Keys still in the ignition, Ross flipped the cage door open and tipped the angry raccoon into the car. He slammed the door, then tossed the cage across the road into the Johnson grass lining the bar ditch.

The silver kids stumbled up the stairs into the graveyard. There was no sign of Big Tolliver yet. Ross walked around behind the Chrysler, head pounding, and stood next to the cracked-open trunk lid. He wanted to be able to get at his shotgun. The heat-stunned rabbits thumped around inside.

Ross heard gravel crunch. He turned to see a gold Mercedes about twenty yards back. The doors swung open as Big Tolliver and Jesus Dempsey got out. Big Tolliver wore a western shirt with silver collar tips and button covers, black jeans and silver-toed ostrich-skin roach stompers. Jesus Dempsey wore a naked-lady Hawaiian shirt, old 501's and a dusty pair of shit kickers.

"Ross Weil, as I live and breathe," said Big Tolliver.

Tolliver and Dempsey still looked the high school football linemen they had been ten years ago down in Azle. They'd beaten the crap out of Ross weekly, just for practice.

Things hadn't changed much. Big Tolliver was based in Aurora now, with three counties to occupy him. Ross got a lot less personal atten-tion. Unfortunately, Big Tolliver was the only person in the area who would front money for Ross's buying and selling habits. Too much buying and not enough selling, in fact. Which was why Ross finally wanted out.

"Big Tolliver." Ross's attempted smile became a queasy wiggle. The Jaegermeister threatened a rapid upward return.

"Fourteen grand, Ross." Big Tolliver shook his head. The police nightstick in his hand caught Ross's attention. "You disappoint me. I like my investments to perform a little better."

Jesus Dempsey muttered the Lord's Prayer, as he had before, during and after every football game back in high school. Ross had it on good authority that Jesus Dempsey muttered the Lord's Prayer during sex.

"My car," Ross said, struggling with both his smile and his gut. "Title's in the glove box. She's yours. Worth twelve grand, at least. I want to settle and get out."

Big Tolliver walked past Ross to strut around the Chrysler. It had hand-rubbed deep purple paint, with a fresh-waxed black vinyl roof. All the chrome had been blacked out, and the glass tinted dark as a limo. The suspension spacers that kept the back of the car off the massively over-sized rear tires gave the body a rake Detroit had never intended. Just looking at the Chrysler filled Ross with a warm surge of pride.

"Get out?" Big Tolliver slammed his nightstick into the driver's side mirror, breaking it off. Ross moaned as Big Tolliver then dented the front left fender. "What? Ain't I treating you *right*?" A headlight was next. The raccoon scrambled madly inside. "Look at this piece of *shit*!" Big Tolliver sounded disgusted. He swung the stick in a two-handed grip onto the front of the hood. "Twelve thousand dollars my ass. You're ripping me off." Another dent, on the right side fender. "You want out, you gotta do better than this, Weil!" Big Tolliver smacked the nightstick against the palm of his other hand, then pointed it at Ross. "You owe fourteen. Car's worth eight thousand, six maybe with this kind of neglect. . . . Is six thousand enough down, Jesus?"

Jesus Dempsey giggled. "It's valley of the shadow of death time, man."

Big Tolliver swung the nightstick into the passenger window. The glass spider-webbed with a sound like the fall of a sack of marbles.

"My car!" howled Ross. He heaved the trunk open and grabbed two damp, torpid rabbits by the ears. He flung the big white bunnies at Jesus Dempsey in a spray of ice chips and rabbit shit.

"Unclean!" shouted Jesus Dempsey as one of the rabbits caught him in the face. He fell backward, struggling with the animal.

Ross grabbed the shotgun from the trunk and pumped the action. The weapon felt strangely light. Wet rabbits spilled out of the trunk, torn between heat exhaustion and panic. Ross stepped around the right side of the car to come face-to-face with Big Tolliver, who had his nightstick cocked back for a blow.

"Hey, Ross," said Big Tolliver in a soft voice, eyes on the gun. "Hold on a minute there."

Conscious of Jesus behind him, Ross dropped and rolled to his right, gun cradled in his arm still pointing at Big Tolliver. "Back off, Tolliver. Where the hell did Dempsey get to?"

As Ross tried to glance over his shoulder, Big Tolliver ducked around the front of the car. Ross stuck his head down, looking under the Chrysler to see Jesus Dempsey kneeling the other side, one hand on the pavement, looking back at him.

Dempsey screeched as Big Tolliver stepped on his hand. The driver door slammed and Big Tolliver hit the starter. The engine rumbled so loudly pebbles jumped under the car.

Big Tolliver laid a scratch with the massive rear tires, coating both Jesus Dempsey and Ross with stinging gravel. Unwilling to shoot at his own car, Ross watched the Chrysler swing out onto the pavement, then spin, flinging yet more rabbits all over the road from the still-opened trunk. Through the windshield he saw the raccoon clawing at Big Tolliver's face. The car lurched forward, spun again and slammed the driver's side door into a telephone pole. The engine died.

Jesus Dempsey sat back eight feet away from Ross and pulled a short-barreled .38 Special from his boot. Ross swung the shotgun around and pulled the trigger. Much to his surprise, the gun made a twanging noise. There was no recoil whatsoever.

Oh, crap, thought Ross.

Jesus Dempsey stared at his chest, where a BB was caught in a fold of his aloha shirt. He laughed. "God, Weil, only you would bring a BB gun to a shootout."

A fat white rabbit hopped by. BB gun in one hand, Ross grabbed the rabbit and jumped to his feet.

"Fine!" he yelled. He whirled the rabbit by its hind legs. "Just shoot me. I've had enough of your crap."

"Okay," said Jesus, still laughing, and raised the pistol.

Ross released the rabbit's feet. Jesus pulled the trigger. The rabbit exploded in a spray of white fur and pink tissue, coating both of them with hot, reeking goop. Jesus laughed so hard he doubled over, slapping his thigh with the pistol. Ross ran forward and whacked Jesus over the head with the BB gun. The plastic stock shattered as Jesus fell face first on to the gravel.

Ross stood, panting, broken BB gun in his hand. He could see a police car topping a distant hill, siren screaming and party lights flashing. Reds and blues, thought Ross. His whole day had been nothing but reds and blues. He really wished he hadn't let the little silver kids polish off the Jaegermeister.

"Excuse me. We have a <click> problem, challenge, opportunity."

It was one of the silver kids, at the top of cemetery stairs. Light blazed from the sky, streaking red and blue. Ross wondered if it was a police helicopter or more of the things he'd seen on the highway.

"Can't find your remote control?" Ross figured it was the last normal conversation he would have for a long time. He was too tired to run, and the cops would be here in a couple of minutes.

The kid waved upward. "No, it was <click> buried, interred, placed as expected. Unfortunately my <click> friends, associates, crewmates have imbibed too much of your <click> potable, liquor, drink. Can you render <click> help, succor, aid?"

Ross still had his baggie of psilocybin spore capsules in his pocket. The cops didn't need to find them. "Here, dude," he said, tossing the baggie upward. "This will clear out that hangover. You guys are pretty small, so, like, one each."

"Our <click> thanks, regards, gratitude for your <click> help, assistance, aid. We would like to repay the <click> favor, kindness, support.

Your <click> car, automobile, conveyance appears damaged. May we offer you a <click> ride, lift, transportation?"

Ross laughed. "Two hours ago, *you* were hitching." He looked down at the rabbit pulp all over his chest. "And things didn't work out like I planned."

"We are fully <click> empowered, enabled, supported now." The red and blue lights wheeled back into the sky behind the kid, like God's police car.

"Dude, that's mighty kind. I appreciate the offer, but I don't really want to go to Canada." He remembered how the kid had refilled his Jaegermeister bottle. "Maybe you could do something about this mess?"

"We will be pleased to fully reward your <click> favor, kindness, support."

It was just like in the movies. The kids really were aliens after all, thought Ross. The red and blue lights spun in the sky, sending a combined beam of yellow light stabbing downward. The little silver kid floated up the beam like it was an elevator. The rabbit pulp separated from Ross's shirt, rising up the beam in little damp sparkles. Busted BB gun at his side, Jesus Dempsey floated up, rotating as he went. Across the street, Big Tolliver stumbled out the car door and rose, head thrown back and legs dangling like someone in a Rapture tract. The Chrysler's sheet metal screeched and popped as the yellow light repaired it. Glass and metal flew across the road to reassemble the mirror while the damaged paint fogged and swirled back into glossy purple. The raccoon and all the rabbits raced through the light toward Ross, mobbing his ankles.

"You all enjoy your anal probes, now," Ross whispered as the UFO clipped the top of a post oak to lurch across the sky in a shower of leaves and twigs.

#

The Wise County Sheriff's Department found Ross on the cemetery steps surrounded by rabbits, a very quiet raccoon in his arms. Since there were no guns in evidence, they told him to get the hell out of their town.

"What do you know?" Ross asked the raccoon as they drove off in the Chrysler. The rabbits filled the back seat, while the raccoon placed its little black hands on the dash. "We're off the hook, and I've still got my car."

He couldn't find the Jaegermeister anywhere, but he didn't really care. The raccoon began grooming Ross's ear.

When he got home, Ross burned his stash and settled down to a quiet, normal life, except for an excess of household pets. As for the Chrysler, it gave excellent mileage and needed no repairs for many years afterward, but the stereo never again played anything except Broadway show tunes sung in incomprehensible whistles and clicks.

PUBLICATION HISTORY

Printed in the United States
27925LVS00001B/205-234